Christine Pullein-Thompson

Strange Riders
at Black Pony Inn

cover illustration by Christine Molan
text illustrations by Gareth Floyd

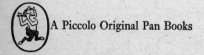
A Piccolo Original Pan Books

First published 1976 by Pan Books Ltd,
Cavaye Place, London SW10.9PG
© Christine Pullein-Thompson 1976
ISBN 0 330 24700 X
Printed in Great Britain by
Richard Clay (The Chaucer Press) Ltd, Bungay, Suffolk

One
Taking the plunge

Dad had summoned us all to the breakfast-room. It was spring, one of those bright sunlit days which seem full of hope so that you can almost feel the sap rising in the trees. We could see the lawns stretching away in front of us and the daffodils tall and yellow under the apple trees. Beyond the lawns were the stables and the straight-railed paddocks, where the first tips of grass were appearing at last through the winter mud.

We knew it was serious. Things had been going wrong for a long time. Creditors had telephoned demanding money, while more and more men had been laid off at the factory. Our house and the paddocks and everything we loved were up for sale. Soon our ponies might be going too. It wasn't anybody's fault. Dad had made a lot of money. He had bought the house and realized a dream he had had for years; now no one wanted his products any more and the dream was over.

Dad had a pile of letters in front of him. I was feeling sick. I had the feeling that this was the end of a chapter in our lives.

I was just twelve with nut-brown hair and blue eyes. Lisa, who was nine, was sitting with Twinkle, our black cat, on her knee. Ben was reading a Western, pretending he didn't care, his fair hair flopping over his eyes, his outgrown trousers barely covering his ankles. James paced the room. Mummy sat with her hands curled round a mug of hot coffee.

'The house isn't selling. The deal has fallen through,' said Dad, putting on his glasses. 'The Arab Company doesn't want it after all, and who else will pay £100,000 and hundreds of pounds in rates every year.'

It was almost a relief to know that the house wasn't sold after all, that we could go on living here with all the last demands in red still coming through the letter box.

'What now, then?' asked Ben, putting down his Western. 'What did they want it for anyway?'

'A guest house for Arab businessmen. I suppose they've found somewhere nearer London,' Dad answered.

'We needn't move then?' cried Lisa with hope in her voice. 'We can stay, can't we? And the ponies can stay too?'

Dad looked at the letters in front of him. 'We can't stay as we are. It isn't possible. I can't go on paying the heating bills and the rates and . . .' he began.

'And the shoeing and the hay bills,' continued James.

'I'll do the mowing,' said Ben. 'And the ponies can live on straw and . . .'

'Can't we run it as something?' suggested Mummy. 'Run it as a guest house and keep everything just the same? Then the rates can come off the income tax and the ponies can give rides and pay for themselves.'

'A children's guest house where children can come when their parents want a change,' I cried.

'We can do up the attics,' Mummy added.

'And teach riding,' cried Lisa.

Suddenly we were all talking at once.

'I can be hall porter and run reception. I can leave school in the autumn,' cried James.

'Old ladies would be more profitable,' said Dad. 'We can't charge them less than twenty-five pounds a week.'

'Twenty for children,' replied Mummy quickly.

'Old ladies eat less than children.'

'We can have both,' said Mummy, pushing her short dark hair behind her ears. 'We can say children over eight are accepted on their own.'

'And the old ladies will look after the children,' cried Lisa, beginning to laugh.

I was feeling excited now. For months life had been difficult with rows over lights being left on, rows over hay bills, oat bills and the cost of petrol for the Land Rover and trailer. For months we had been living beyond our means. Now we would all be helping to pay the bills. I saw hordes of children arriving with suitcases. I saw myself taking them up to the newly painted attics, escorting them for rides. I thought of the house full of laughter with twenty to dinner in the long dining-room and a log fire burning in the huge fireplace. I had been wanting a job for ages, but there was nothing but the local paper round which James had bagged years ago. Now we all had jobs. Our lean days were over.

We made plans. We rushed from room to room counting how many beds would go in each. The attics were full of cobwebs and old suitcases. There were three rooms and we reckoned each would take six children.

'Eighteen children at twenty pounds a week each. How much is that?' cried Ben.

'Three hundred and sixty pounds a week,' replied James.

'But they will have to be fed,' said Dad.

'But we can charge for riding,' argued Ben.

'But they will need someone to cook and sweep up after them,' said Mummy.

'Perhaps they will bring their own ponies,' suggested Lisa. 'I don't want my darling Jigsaw worked to death.'

'We don't need to make a lot of money, just enough to go on living here,' said Mummy quietly.

'And employ a gardener, three grooms and a butler,' added Ben, who has disgusting ideas of grandeur.

Later we wandered round to the stables, which had once known better days. We had turned our ponies out earlier, but they came across the field when they saw us, hoping for a second breakfast. James doesn't ride. He's tall and dark and rather vague and just sixteen. He had stayed behind to help Mummy count the sheets in the airing cupboard.

'I hope they don't mind being ridden by strangers,' said Ben now, patting his dark brown, part-bred Welsh cob, Solitaire.

Jigsaw was small and piebald with a clever face and a crooked patch of black above his left eye. Once he had pulled a coster-monger's cart and he had a quick trot which had won Lisa a host of trotting races. He had spring, too, and could jump almost anything. He was the apple of Lisa's eye. If she could, she would have taken him to bed with her like a teddy bear.

Then there was Limpet, the little black which we had all grown out of in turn. Once he had been our only pony and we had fought over him, fallen off him and generally mismanaged him. My mare was a grey with a head which pulled at your heart-strings. She was dappled like an old-fashioned rocking horse and I had called her Lorraine after the poem by Charles Kingsley.

'Four ponies won't go far with eighteen children,' I said now.

'So we may have to buy some more,' suggested Ben optimistic-ally.

'From the horse sanctuary or the market,' cried Lisa. I saw the yard full of horses, greys and bays, blacks, chestnuts and roans.

'They must be safe,' I said. 'We don't want any accidents.'

'What shall we call the place?' asked Ben. 'The Great Ranch Guest House.'

'Don't be mad,' I answered. 'It's going to be a guest house, not a ranch.'

'Can't we call it The Little Pony Guest House?' Lisa asked.

'No, it's pathetic. It makes it sound little, and it isn't,' replied Ben.

We sat on the rail fence trying to think of a name, and there was sunlight everywhere and life seemed lit with hope.

None of us stopped to consider the trials and tribulations which might lie ahead, the piles of washing up, horrible children, unmanageable ponies, unpleasant or mad old ladies, heaps of dirty clothes. At that moment everything looked as golden as the day. All it needed was a name.

'We must have horse or pony in it,' Ben said. 'Then even if

8

we get bags of old ladies, they will be nice horsey ones, you know, old experts who can teach us lots about horses, titled ladies.'

'Titled ladies! Honestly, you get worse every day,' I replied.

'Inn sounds much more old world than guest house,' Ben said. 'Guest house is genteel.'

'Let's call it Black Pony Inn after Limpet. After all, he taught us everything,' I said.

'Super,' cried Lisa.

'Smashing,' said Ben.

We rushed indoors with the suggestion, but Mummy had a pile of silver in front of her and Dad was going through the demands in red. They seemed preoccupied. Dad just said, 'Go away.' And Mummy said, 'Tell your father I'm going to sell all the silver. There's no point in keeping it. Nasty children will nick it.'

'Nasty children!' I cried.

'Yes, we will have some for sure,' replied Mummy.

'But what will we eat with when all the silver's gone?' asked Ben.

'Cheaper cutlery.'

I remembered that Mummy had come from a well-off background, whereas Dad had made his way by hard work and enterprise. She had inherited the silver. Ben looked at it with dismay. He had turned quite pale. He loved things like silver.

'The money from the silver will buy sheets and blankets, and we need a deep freeze and bags of food from the supermart,' she said. 'We are lucky to have it to sell. The sheets and blankets will cost a fortune.'

I went upstairs to see what I could sell. My bedroom looked towards the stables. It was large, with an armchair and a desk as well as a bed and lots of cupboards. I had an idea it wouldn't be mine much longer. I found some outgrown clothes, and a pile of books which I had meant to keep for my children if I had any. They might buy a bag of pony cubes, I thought without much hope, and heaven knows the ponies need more food. It had been a disastrous year, hay had gone up to seventy pounds a ton and oats to a hundred. Now we had no hay left, only oat straw and a bit of hard feed, and the Easter holidays were just beginning. I put my books into a suitcase and thought how lovely it would be to be rich again, to be able to buy bags and bags of pony cubes and tons of oats; to buy bran and linseed again and to have our ponies shod when they needed it instead of waiting until their shoes were dropping off. I was ready to work myself to death for it if necessary. We needed new clothes too. Ben's jacket was half-way up his arms, Lisa's crash cap was frayed in front and I had grown out of my riding coat six months ago. As for James, he had taken to buying his clothes from the OXFAM shop.

The next few days we worked almost non-stop, clearing out the attics, painting them, spring-cleaning the whole house. Our arms and legs ached. At night we slept like logs, too tired even to dream. Yet in a strange way we were happy, happier than we had been for months. We seemed to be doing something concrete at last. We were no longer sitting on the fence watching our lives crumbling about us. We were fighting back at last. We were certain that the awful days of our genteel poverty were over, that we were going to save ourselves, and would never have to ask Dad for money again. We were convinced that in a few weeks money would be flowing into our house like gold in a gold rush.

We hardly rode at all because we had no time and because our ponies looked so awful with deep poverty marks round their quarters and their coats falling out.

Mummy received nearly four hundred pounds for the silver, because some of it was Georgian, and she bought two new beds with it with first-class mattresses for the old ladies and some cheaper second-hand beds for the children, and a pile of nylon sheets and pillow cases and cellular blankets.

My clothes fetched three pounds and my books two, so I was able to buy a whole hundredweight of oats and a few pony cubes. Ben sold his tape recorder and bought himself a jacket because he said he must look smart if he was to wait on old ladies.

By the middle of April we were ready, and Dad suggested we should advertise in the local paper which was bought over a wide area and wouldn't cost as much as advertising in the national press. He was still gloomy. More men had been laid off and he was now working on the floor himself instead of supervising from his office. He came home late every night with a case full of work. The lines had deepened on his face and he looked much older.

None of us dared ask him for anything, and there were dreadful rows because Ben would play his transistor full blast.

The spring grass had really come and at least the ponies were beginning to look fatter. Ben and I drew up the advertisement on the kitchen table because James and Mummy were out stocking up with food. It went like this:

> GET AWAY FROM IT ALL AT THE BLACK PONY INN
> Middle Hampton. Sumptuous weekends in the
> country at moderate rates. Long-term guests.
> Unaccompanied children over eight accepted.
> Full board £20–25 a week.
> RIDING: Ring Middle Hampton 2222 for details

We looked at it for a long time before we posted it in the little red post-box near the village shop. In three days it would be published. The house was polished, the tack was clean; we had even brushed our shoes and clothes.

'We've taken the plunge,' said Ben as we walked home together. 'For better or for worse.'

'Like marriage,' said Lisa, catching us up.

'It's the only way. Whatever happens afterwards we must remember that there was no other way,' replied Ben.

Middle Hampton is small with cottages built of brick and flint. Our house was once the Manor House. It stands a little way away from the other houses looking towards distant hills.

'We need a sign now,' Ben said. 'I'll make one straight away. Otherwise no one will find us.'

'And an arrow,' I added.

I couldn't believe it was happening, that we had reached this stage at last. Ben was running now; we were all running.

'I know where there's a bit of suitable wood,' he cried. 'I wish I could draw.'

'James can,' I yelled. 'Ask James.'

'We must put "guest house" somewhere, or people will think we sell drinks,' Ben replied, breaking into a walk.

'Like a pub?' I asked.

'Yes, we can put BLACK PONY INN, and then under the picture of Limpet's head, *Unlicensed Guest House* in smaller letters. James can do the head and I will do the lettering,' said Ben.

'And we can have a wooden arrow further up pointing the way,' cried Lisa. 'Or a hand. What about a hand?'

'Yes, a hand,' cried Ben and we started running again as though success and happiness were running ahead of us waiting to be caught.

Two
'I'm crazy about horses'

After the advertisement came out, we waited a whole day for something to happen. The house seemed to be waiting, too.

Dad said, 'I knew it wouldn't work.'

Mummy said, 'Give it time.'

'I'm frightened,' cried Lisa. 'Supposing I hate the children.'

'There aren't going to be any children,' replied Ben.

I thought of the sheets and the blankets, of the deep freeze stocked with food which we would never eat on our own. Then there was a knock on the door and we all jumped, thinking that it must be a prospective guest. But it was only old Colonel Jones from the village come to tell us that we needed planning permission before we could erect a sign.

'To the devil with planning permission,' replied Dad. 'You know it takes months to get a decision from them; and we can't afford to wait.'

'They will make you take it down. I'm on the Parish Council. I know what's going on,' replied Colonel Jones.

Mummy offered him a cup of tea or a drink, but he said that it would look like bribery if he accepted.

Outside it was raining, and no one had written or telephoned and the day was nearly gone.

'They'll make you take it down,' muttered Colonel Jones, going out the way he had come.

'Who's "they"?' asked Lisa, chewing a pencil.

'The District Council,' replied Dad.

'If they touch my sign I'll kill them,' said Ben.

*

The next day the telephone rang. We were eating breakfast – bowls of cereal, toast and marmalade. Ben answered. He stood holding the phone and smiling.

'It's lots of children,' said Lisa hopefully.

'It's the District Council demanding immediate removal of the sign,' replied James.

'It's someone demanding to be paid,' I said gloomily. After ages of suspense, Ben put down the telephone.

'It's about an old lady,' he said, his voice thick with disappointment. 'Her daughter wants us to have her for three months while she's with her husband in South Africa. She keeps on talking.'

Mummy went to the phone.

'I knew it would be like this,' said Ben gloomily.

'I feel sick with excitement,' Lisa said.

'We'll have to wait on her, and she'll hate us,' continued Ben. 'She'll criticize our clothes, everything.'

'She'll want breakfast in bed,' said James. 'And Harriet will have to take her out in a wheel-chair.'

'She's eighty,' Ben told us.

'That's terribly old,' cried Lisa.

'She'll be senile,' said James.

'What's senile?' asked Lisa.

'They are all coming round to look in half an hour,' said Mummy, putting down the phone. 'The old lady sounds a dear, she does really. She says she likes a full house, and she wants to do the garden. Think of that at eighty!'

We began to feel better.

'One old lady, just one old lady,' said Ben.

'I like old ladies,' exclaimed James. 'I've always wanted lots of grannies.'

But now the telephone was ringing again. We fell over each other trying to reach it. James got there first.

'It's a mother this time. She's got a terribly bossy voice and her daughter rides,' he said, handing the phone to Mummy again while the person at the other end went on talking.

'It's a success, it's going to be a success,' shrieked Lisa.

'Don't count your chickens before they are hatched,' warned James.

'Well, there is a bus service but it only runs once a week,' Mummy was saying. 'No, there's no station. Yes, it's quite isolated.'

'Perhaps she's bringing dogs,' suggested Ben.

'We'll do our best of course, but it's not a prison,' Mummy continued.

'A convict, we're going to have a convict,' muttered James.

'Yes, four ponies, two are quite large. Yes, almost unlimited riding,' Mummy said.

'A riding maniac,' said Ben.

'Are you sure you don't want to see the place first? I mean Mary might not like us,' Mummy continued.

'We are going to have a difficult girl. She must not be allowed to disappear alone,' Mummy said, putting down the receiver. 'We must hide the car keys. Do you think we'll manage?'

'What's the matter with her?' asked Ben.

'She's in love with an impossible boy. And her mother thinks riding will take her mind off him.'

'Oh no!' cried Ben.

'How old is she?' I wanted to know.

'Thirteen. She's coming tonight complete with luggage. Her mother seems in a great hurry to be rid of her. She's paying five pounds extra for special care.'

'Gosh, that's fifty pounds a week already,' cried Ben.

'Can she ride?' I asked.

'Yes. She's very keen. She used to have a pony of her own.'

'Bags take her riding then,' I said.

The telephone rang once more. I answered it. The voice at the other end was decidedly American. I fetched Mummy. We had made up the old lady's bed and Mary's by this time and put the kettle on and had tea cups ready for our prospective customers. Mummy talked for ages.

At last she stopped. 'We have a boy coming too with an Anglo–Arab horse called Apollo which cost a thousand pounds. Can you have a loose-box ready?' she asked.

'Yes of course,' I said.

'His parents are going back to an apartment in the States, in Washington, and he won't go without his horse. So they want him to stay till they have things sorted out. He'll go to boarding school and they are paying in advance.' She sounded tired, as though now suddenly she saw the problems which lay ahead. Lisa put her arms round her.

'Don't worry, it's going to be all right,' she said. 'Mary will fall in love with Ben or James and Harriet can look after the American boy. Don't worry, Mummy darling. Just keep calm.'

Ben and I bedded down a loose-box. We didn't talk much.

'There're going to be a lot of strange people around here,' Ben said at last. 'I hope we can cope.'

'So do I,' I replied, shaking up the straw.

Later we heard the front doorbell. 'Which one is it?' I asked.

'The old lady, I expect,' replied Ben.

Presently we saw her walking round the garden with Mummy and James, admiring everything. She was small, like people were years ago, and looked incredibly old. We could hear her say, 'I love gardening. I shall soon have things straight. And if you want the spuds done, I'll do them.'

'But you're paying,' Mummy replied. 'You mustn't work all the time.'

She came to look at the horses and admired them, too. 'And what a lovely stable yard!' she exclaimed. 'When I have time I'll weed it for you.'

'She's sweet,' said James later. 'A really nice old lady. She won't be any trouble.'

Mary came later with a tall, thin-lipped mother in tweeds. Mary wore nail varnish and was slim and tall for her age. She didn't say much, though I saw her looking hard at James and Ben.

Ben hardly spoke three words to her, but her mother never

stopped talking. 'You will like it here, Mary,' she said. 'You'll be able to get up early every morning and go riding just as you did when you had Trixie. And you can help with the mucking out, too. You'll never have a dull moment, will you dear?' Mary remained aloof and detached. I felt that she despised us all and would hate every moment of life with us. I prayed that she would not come, but after a time I heard Mummy saying, 'We'll do our best then, Mrs Harris. But I'm not making any promises.' And Mary looked round and smiled, a nasty, secret smile.

Later we had tea together in the kitchen. The old lady, who was called Mrs Mills, poured out. 'I'll have a mug,' she offered. 'I hate cups and saucers.'

She was very deaf and kept shouting, 'What?' and 'Oh dear, I must get a deaf aid; you all mutter so.'

Mary said, 'Whatever do you do all day here buried in the country, miles from everywhere? I should go mad.'

'We ride,' replied Ben. 'And if you don't, I should beat it because you'll be bored stiff.'

And then there was a knock on the back door and a voice said, 'May we come in?'

The voice was unmistakably American. 'Yes, of course,' cried Mummy. 'But you should have come the front way.'

Mrs Mills got out some more cups and started to fill them with tea.

'It sure is a cute place here. What do you say, Paul?'

The father was large, with success written all over him. The mother was square-shaped, with short greying hair cut in a fringe. Paul was tubby with a scrubbed look about him. His hair was short and curly and he was wearing grey trousers and a blazer with a crest on it.

'Sure, great,' he answered. 'But it's the stables I want to see. Have you a box ready for my chestnut?'

I nodded.

'The name's Armstrong. We're sure glad to meet you,' announced the father.

We shook hands. 'Show Paul the stables,' Mummy said.

The box was ready. We had even filled a bucket of water and a haynet. And Ben had spent ages banking up the straw round the sides. It really did look lovely.

Paul breathed a sigh of relief. 'It sure looks great. Can I pin his name on the door?' he asked.

'If you like,' I said, 'but you'll have to take down Limpet's name.'

'He cost nearly three thousand dollars. I've got a chart here saying what he needs to eat. Can I pin it up somewhere?'

'Yes, in the tack room,' I said, thinking that he was certainly keen on pinning things up.

'Have you got him outside?' Ben asked.

'No, we've still got to fetch him. Can I see your horses? This place is sure okay,' Paul continued. 'I couldn't stand going back to an apartment in the States. I'm crazy about horses. How about you?'

'Us too,' I said.

'You wait till you see him, he's some horse,' he said.

His parents were approaching now. They walked round talking, saying, 'This will be great for Paul. Now about his school, can you take him back and fetch him at half-term?'

'Yes, we'll do that,' Mummy answered, looking dazed as though too much had happened too quickly and she was still trying to get things straight in her mind. 'He's having your bedroom, Harriet,' she said, 'because yours has a washbasin and he wants one facing the stables, so that he can see Apollo.'

It was my first sacrifice for our paying guests. I tried not to feel resentful. Mrs Mills had one spare room and Mary had the other. The attics were still empty. I supposed I would be sent there to sleep alone. 'Sure you don't mind?' asked Mrs Armstrong. 'You're not upset, dear?'

'No,' I said. 'Not at all.'

'Okay then, all set,' said Mr Armstrong. 'Paul, you're going to be real happy here, aren't you? You're sure?'

Paul nodded, looking at me, then to Ben and back again.

'It will be great,' he said. 'I feel it in my bones.'

I wanted to say, 'Touch wood,' but I didn't.

Afterwards I wished I had. It might have altered things, saved us the horrible moments which lay ahead unknown to any of us.

Mr Armstrong wrote Mummy a cheque in the large sitting-room which has deep armchairs and lots of reproduction furniture and a carpet which cost a thousand pounds. It is the only smart room in the house and we had decided to keep it for occasions like this.

'That's three months in advance – ten pounds a week for Apollo and twenty for Paul and plenty more for gasoline. I want you to give Paul his pocket money too – that's five pounds a week,' he said, putting his gold pen back into his pocket.

Mummy looked at the cheque, then folded it up. 'Right you are,' she said.

They left by the front door and somehow the house seemed smaller and more humdrum when they had gone. I can't explain why – they just made everything seem bigger, greater, more important.

Twilight had come now. It was too late to ride. We could hear Dad returning. Mrs Mills had washed up and was peeling potatoes for supper.

Mary was sitting in the study, watching television.

I set the table for the supper. I was upset at losing my bedroom. It was full of my things. But it would be even worse when the guests started riding Lorraine. I wished that Mary was different. She was old for her age and smart and I had wanted a girl of my own age in faded jeans and an old sweater. I couldn't imagine Mary mucking out even if she had once had a pony called Trixie. I supposed Ben and I would muck out Apollo's box, taking it in turns. We would probably have to groom him too, and Paul might expect his tack cleaned as well.

Supper was laid at last. Mummy appeared and put her arms around me. 'I hope you don't mind losing your room. We've got two more guests coming, two little girls. I want you to share the attics with them. Their mother has gone into hospital and their father's had a car crash. It's a desperate case. They like riding. They can ride Limpet . . .' she said looking into my face. 'You don't mind, do you? Apollo's ten pounds a week is to go to you and Ben to spend on horse food, and so will any riding money. Okay?'

'Okay,' I said. 'But what are the girls called?'

'Phillipa and Georgie. They sound sweet. Their grannie's bringing them. They're only here for two weeks, that's all. Do cheer up.'

'When's Apollo coming?' I wanted to know.

'Tomorrow in the morning. I want you to take out Mary early. She'll have to ride Solitaire, won't she?' Mummy asked.

'Yes.'

Ben was beating the gong, which had always stood in the hall but had never been used before. Mary demanded her supper by the television and James took it to her on a tray. I think we were all tired, though Lisa kept talking, saying that Paul was handsome and Mary nasty and that the two new girls would be her friends and that she would teach them to ride whatever Ben said.

Later I lay in bed, trying to imagine the future, thinking that it was my last night in my own bed, wondering whether it would ever be my room again. Lisa slept in the little room next to Mummy and Daddy. Ben and James slept at the back of the house in two rooms which looked towards the village.

Then Ben knocked on the door and came in. He sat on my bed and said, 'Think, ten pounds a week to spend on what we like. We can buy oats and a martingale for Solitaire and the nylon type of rug you've always wanted for Lorraine. We're going to be rich, you realize that, don't you? – rich! And it won't be Dad's money this time. It will belong to all of us.'

'Yes, but money isn't everything,' I said.

Ben stared at me. 'It's a heck of a lot,' he said. 'Did you want to leave here? To go back to living in a street, in a row of houses . . . ? We are making a success. Everything's going like we dreamed it would. What more do you want?'

'Nothing,' I answered. 'I just wish Mary was nice, that's all.'

'Well, I love money,' said Ben, going out without shutting the door.

I thought, we will go on taking desperate cases because Mummy is so generous, and the house will soon be full of selfish Marys and decrepit old ladies, and it won't be any fun at all. I could hear Ben now, arguing with James on the stairs, and Dad letting Twinkle out.

I shouted, 'You didn't shut my door!' but no one paid the least attention.

Trying to sleep, I decided that when I was grown up I would school horses, turning three-hundred-pound animals into jumpers worth thousands of pounds, and I shall have a big house with lots of paddocks, I thought, and a proper jumping saddle with a spring tree, and my own bedroom with photographs of horses all over the walls, and no one will turn me out of it. And if I marry, it will be to someone horsey, so that we can go to shows together and perhaps to America and then the Olympics. And when I fell asleep at last, it was with imagined cheers ringing in my ears, and with the Union Jack being raised in a great arena and my name in all the papers of the world.

Three
A quarrel

I got up at half past seven in the morning.

The sky was full of mad, scurrying clouds blowing hither and thither, like scraps of torn paper.

Mummy was getting breakfast in the dining-room, putting out packets of cereals, spoons, sugar and milk. Mrs Mills had already had her breakfast. We soon learned that she never waited for anyone but got her own – a vast mug of coffee, toast and marmalade. Already she was more like a relation than a guest. James was still in bed and so was Mary. The rest of us went down to the stables.

We had left the ponies out last night for the first time since October. There were four loose-boxes and six old-fashioned stalls with Staffordshire brick floors, iron mangers and hay racks, and partitions with brass knobs on them like old bedsteads. There were still cobbles in part of the yard, dating back years. They made me imagine the horses which might have trodden them down – the proud carriage-horses, the master's hunters, a little pony which pulled a governess cart. Everything felt lovely in the early morning, fresh and new and spring-like.

Ben put clean water in Apollo's box. 'Everything must be perfect,' he said.

I loved the yard, the lovely smells of straw and hay and horse. I sat on the fence and looked at it and thought how lucky we were to be here in the spring sunlight with our ponies grazing in the paddock and the whole summer before us.

Ben was looking at the garden. 'Next year we will have a swimming pool, heated, of course,' he said.

He was always optimistic. He made everything seem possible, even the wildest dreams. Lisa had her arms round Jigsaw's thick black and white neck, her face buried in his mane.

For a moment everything was still and beautiful and I thought, if only everything could stay like this for ever, if only we never grew older, just stayed the same.

Then we heard a lorry coming along the road and a minute later Ben was shouting 'Horsebox!' and opening the yard gate. And we could see Paul Armstrong's clean, scrubbed face looking at us through the cab window. It was a beautiful horsebox, all varnished wood and padded partitions; the sort which costs pounds and pounds to hire.

Apollo had a race and snip and three white socks and a flaxen mane and tail. He was almost a palomino with thin legs and small hoofs and the carriage of an Arab. He wasn't my sort of horse, but you could see that Paul worshipped him. His legs were bandaged, his tail covered with a tail guard. His elegant rug had Paul's initials in gold on one corner – PLA.

Apollo walked down the ramp and into his loose-box like a prince.

'You're early,' Ben said.

'My cases are in the cab, wait a sec.' Paul was dressed in breeches and boots and a tweed jacket. He had brought three cases, all with his initials on them in gold lettering, too. Once I had thought we were rich, but we had never had gold initials or a thousand-pound pony. Paul tipped the driver two pounds.

Apollo started eating his hay as we stood and looked at him over the door.

'He's some horse, isn't he?' asked Paul. 'You understand now why I couldn't go back to the States without him?'

I took off his leg bandages and tail guard while Ben held him. Paul watched. You could see he was used to being waited on. I wanted to say, 'Why don't you give a hand?' But I remembered that we were being paid ten pounds a week to look after his pony.

Apollo was very well behaved and stood with his eyes half-closed meanwhile.

'He's certainly no trouble,' said Ben. 'He's far quieter than any of ours.'

'He's sure good-natured. He's the same to ride,' replied Paul.

Mary was up when we wandered indoors for breakfast.

'I got her up,' James said. 'I just went on banging on the door until she couldn't stand it any more.'

She was wearing flared jeans and a sweater.

'I never get up before twelve at home,' she said.

'We must have some rules here,' Mummy replied. 'Even the best hotels don't go on serving breakfast for ever.'

'I never eat breakfast at home,' answered Mary, 'so I shan't eat it here.'

We looked at one another, hating her, knowing she was going to spoil the rest of the holidays.

'I want to ride this morning,' she continued. 'Can I take which I like?'

'No. Harriet will ride with you,' Mummy said.

Daddy had left for the factory. I wished he was here to manage Mary. I didn't want to ride alone with her. I could see her galloping along roads, ignoring me, saying, 'You're only a kid,' and, 'So what!'

It was nine o'clock now. Mrs Mills was cleaning saucepans just as though she was a hired help. I took the dirty plates out and stacked them in the dishwasher. Paul hurried down to the stables to look at Apollo.

'Is he afraid he'll melt or something?' James asked.

'He loves him, that's all,' I said.

Lisa ran after him shrieking, 'Wait for me.'

Mummy said, 'I'm going to advertise for some help. I can't cope alone.'

'Let me do the beds,' offered Mrs Mills. 'I love making beds.'

I said, 'Coming?' to Mary and we went down to the stables together. Ben had caught Solitaire and was grooming him. He looked at Mary with dislike. 'If she hurts Solitaire, I'll kill her,' he muttered.

He didn't mean it, of course. But I knew how he felt. It's one thing to let someone you know ride your pony, quite another to let someone you hate.

Lorraine was clean. I tacked her up and waited. Paul was talking to Apollo. 'He needs a day to settle down, doesn't he?' he asked. 'He's still half asleep from the journey.'

Ben nodded. 'You can't be too careful with a horse like him,' he said with laughter behind his eyes.

Ben held the stirrup while Mary mounted.

'He goes best on a loose rein,' he said.

'I don't need your advice. I can ride. I won a Best Rider class when I was eight,' she said.

Ben looked as though he was praying as I led the way out of the yard.

We rode across the common and down into the beech woods where everything was bright and green and new. Spring seemed everywhere. Birds were singing in trees, new calves lay by their mothers in green fields. We didn't talk much, but I could see that Mary could ride. She rode easily on a loose rein and Solitaire strode out, his ears pricked, his eyes shining.

Finally I asked her where she lived and she replied, 'In Sussex, in a ghastly place full of rich people's houses.'

And then I said, 'What happened to Trixie?' and for a long time she didn't answer, just looked straight ahead into the distance.

'Mother sold her,' she said finally. 'She was a grey like yours – a fabulous pony. But I would rather not talk about it. Can we canter?'

'Okay,' I said and saw with a twinge of envy that she rode better than I did, far better.

When we drew rein, I asked her if she missed her boy friend, but she said that she would rather not talk about that, either. 'You're only a kid,' she continued. 'You wouldn't understand.'

'I'm nearly as old as you,' I replied.

'In years perhaps, but in other ways you're much younger. You still dress like a child, don't you? And talk like one. You're years and years behind me,' she said.

I knew it was true, but I didn't want to grow up. I wanted to stay eleven or twelve for ever. I didn't want the responsibilities, the discothèques, the agonies of being a teenager. I couldn't explain it. But I just wanted to go on as I was. I looked at her superior, made-up face and hated her.

We were nearly home again now. We didn't talk. She was probably hating me, too. I noticed that she wore a cross round her neck and her ears were pierced for earrings. I still envied her the way she rode.

When we reached the stable yard, she threw her reins to Ben. 'I like your horse, but he's too much on the forehand. He needs more balancing exercises,' she said. 'I'll school him for nothing if you like.'

'No, thank you,' replied Ben, running up the stirrups, hating her as much as I did.

As she walked away, we looked at each other and tried to laugh. 'She rides beautifully, you needn't have worried,' I said.

'She a horrible little madam,' said Ben. 'And there's something odd about her. She's horrible on purpose.'

'She's hating everyone,' I answered. 'I don't believe she's really that bad.'

'She's a sadist then,' said Ben.

The weather was changing. It was almost too hot for spring and yet the sky was filling with clouds, and there were flies already buzzing round the ponies' heads.

'She's going to spoil the whole holidays, I feel it in my bones,' I said.

The two little girls had arrived when we went indoors. They were playing with Lisa. They both had long hair tied back behind their ears and small faces shaped like monkeys' faces. They laughed and chattered and I could see that everybody was going to like them. Mrs Mills had already found a game of ludo and they all planned to play together after lunch.

Mummy looked relaxed and happy. Paul was reading a book of Ben's called *Stable Management and How to Cope* by Brigadier Smallpiece.

Nobody talked much at lunch. Mummy said, 'What about this afternoon, Mary? Have you any plans? How about a walk? Or are you going to ride again?'

'I shall write letters,' Mary said. 'And my hair needs washing; I have plenty to do.'

'I'll take Georgie and Phillipa riding later if they like,' I offered.

They bobbed up and down in their chairs shrieking, 'Hurray,' and 'Yes, please,' while Paul put his hands over his ears and Mary said, 'Excuse me,' and left the table.

'You had better go soon, before the storm breaks,' suggested Mummy.

We all cleared the table. I went outside to catch Limpet. The dark skies seemed nearer. It was as though everything were waiting for something. I wondered how long we would be able to stand Mary. Paul was irritating, but Mary seemed out to annoy everyone. No one had mucked out Apollo, so I fetched a barrow and tools and cleaned out his box. Then I caught Limpet and groomed her. After that I went indoors to find Georgie and Phillipa, and found Ben having a row with Mary in the hall.

He had bumped into her on the stairs, and she had called him a stupid fat lout. It was one of those rows which start over nothing and go on and on.

Ben should have held his tongue, but he isn't like that – it's blow for blow as far as he's concerned and no holds barred.

'Well, you're a stupid old cow,' he cried. 'And a sadist, and if you think you're going to ride my pony again, you're not.'

'I pay to be here,' shrieked Mary, 'and I will do what I like. It's a pretty crabby place anyway and you're the most boring people I've ever met.'

Mummy came into the hall at that moment. 'Go to your room at once, Ben,' she said.

He stood glaring at her, defying both of them.

'I always get the blame, don't I?' he said at last, going back upstairs.

'I think you had better leave tomorrow, Mary. I don't think we can cope with you. I'll talk to your mother again tonight,' Mummy said.

There was a horrible silence while Mary turned pale. 'He bumped into me,' she said. 'He should have apologized.'

'You were screaming like a fish wife,' Mummy retorted, 'and we don't want fish wives here.'

'I can't go home.'

'You will have to go somewhere else then.'

Mummy went back into the kitchen, shutting the door after her.

Mary looked at me as though she wanted to say something, but I was too angry to speak, for she had spoilt the whole day as far as I was concerned and had called my brother a fat lout. I didn't want to be her friend, not now or ever.

'My mother pays five pounds extra a week for special care,' she said. 'And I'm not getting it.'

'What do you expect?' I asked. 'Breakfast in bed?'

'Extras,' she muttered.

'You're mad,' I said. 'Goodbye.'

I slammed the hall door after me and found Phillipa and Georgie playing ludo with Mrs Mills in what used to be called the nursery. They found their crash caps and boots and ran ahead to the stables. Limpet loves small children and he behaved beautifully. I took them each in turn and we did bending and I made a practice garden path out of sticks and they rode down it. Then we practised potato race and reining back. And nothing awful happened in spite of distant rolls of thunder and Paul watching over the gate.

After that we cleaned the tack together and they told me about their guinea pigs which were called Spick and Span.

I didn't want to go back into the house, but James came down to the stables and said that it was tea and what had I done to Mary: she was crying her eyes out.

'What have I done? I like that,' I answered.

Mary had tea in her bedroom. I suppose she didn't want anyone to see that she had been crying. Later, Dad came home and talked to her for a long time and it was finally agreed she could stay on.

'She's just a mixed up kid,' Dad said, 'Basically there's nothing wrong with her. It's just a difficult age.'

'She's just a sadist, that's all,' said Ben.

'And thoroughly unpleasant,' I added.

'And mean and vain and horrible,' shrieked Lisa.

We were in the sitting-room all together for once without a single guest in sight. Then Mary came in quickly and stared at us and said, 'I heard what you said just now, every word. I was listening at the door.' And then she rushed out again.

Dad went after her and I went red and Ben said several words which we are definitely not allowed to use. And Mummy said, 'That's that then.'

Then the telephone started to ring. It was for Paul and I fetched him from where he was watching television and he talked for ages.

'They rang up to say goodbye,' he said, hanging up at last. 'They wanted to know if Apollo was okay. They said something funny too; they said, look out for letter bombs and don't take lifts from strange men. What do you think they meant?'

'They were just being funny, that's all,' Mummy answered.

'They've never said it before.'

Outside, the storm was breaking at last. Lightning lit up the room, crash after crash of thunder followed. Lisa screamed and hid her face.

Dad came back. 'I've calmed her down. She doesn't want to leave. You must all try to be kinder to her,' he said. 'Her parents are separated. She's in her own private hell and very mixed up.'

'She'll have us all mixed up soon,' said Ben. 'You know insanity can be catching.'

'Shut up,' replied Dad. 'She's paying extra. She's entitled to extra treatment. She's ordered steak tonight and she must have it.'

'But we haven't got any,' Mummy said.

In the end we had braised steak. We talked about gymkhanas all through supper and suddenly another day had gone. I played with Georgie and Phillipa before they went to bed. The three of us slept together in the first attic, which had pale-blue walls and curtains with prancing horses on them. It looked out at the back of the house on big elm trees where squirrels played and grey wood pigeons nested. Phillipa and Georgie loved it. They kept saying: 'It's tons better than our rooms in our horrid little doll's house.'

Before I went to bed I wandered down to the stables and everything looked new and clear and sparkling after the storm. The ponies came across the field to me in the dusk and nuzzled my pockets and Apollo whinnied from his loose-box. The storm was still lingering in the sky. Dark clouds lay on the horizon and there was the occasional distant rumble. Ben came down and filled up Apollo's bucket and said, 'Everything all right?'

'I think so.' He was being nicer than usual. Usually we quarrelled a good deal, but having guests had somehow made us better friends.

'I wish I could sleep here,' I said.

'Same here,' he agreed.

Apollo looked sleepy but otherwise well. We went inside his box and ran our hands down his legs and checked that his haynet was full. And Ben said, 'Except for Mary I think we are making a success of it, don't you?'

I said, 'We've only just started. Sometimes I'm frightened. Supposing burglars came to stay or murderers?'

'Why should they?'

'Or Apollo got colic and died.'

'Don't be silly and neurotic. Everything is going marvellously. Why spoil it?' asked Ben.

'I don't know what we will do when Mrs Mills leaves,' I said next.

'Get another old lady to pay twenty-five pounds and do all the work,' replied Ben, laughing.

I didn't want to go indoors. I had the feeling that disaster lay just round the corner. I checked that the field gate was shut. Apollo was lying down now and I checked that his door was bolted top and bottom and shut the yard gate.

'Crikey, you *are* nervous tonight,' Ben said.

'I'm afraid we are going to be struck by lightning,' I replied. 'Listen, the storm is just waiting to come back.'

The air felt tense and humid and the horses in the field were restless. We went indoors together. 'I shan't sleep,' I said. 'I feel upset. I suppose it's Mary.'

Lisa was playing in the attic. I chased her downstairs to her own room. Georgie and Phillipa wouldn't stop talking. I heard Dad putting Twinkle out, locking up. I heard the roar of distant aircraft and dogs barking down in the village. When I fell asleep, I dreamed that I was riding towards a precipice with Mary. She was wearing a head-scarf and as we drew near she tried to push me over. I woke up to find I was sweating and that my bedclothes were on the floor. The sky was still rumbling. I thought, the Gods are angry, and fell asleep again.

Four
'The field's empty'

It was daylight when I wakened again and Lisa was in the room screaming at me, 'They've gone. All of them. The field's empty.' My eyes were full of sleep, my hair tangled.

'Who? What?'

I saw now that Paul was standing behind her. 'Apollo's gone too,' he said.

I leapt out of bed. I could feel my heart banging inside me, my pulse racing. 'I checked everything. Where's Ben?' I yelled.

'Getting up.'

Phillipa and Georgie woke up and started asking questions which no one had time to answer.

I pulled clothes on over my pyjamas, tore downstairs, found my boots. Ben was just ahead of me, still in his dressing gown.

Apollo's door was open, the field gate was open, the gate into the road was open. I wanted to scream or cry, but no sound came and no tears.

'Look at the tyre marks,' shouted Ben. 'Look!'

'It could be thieves, cattle rustlers,' I said. My voice came out small and croaky. We knew about horse and cattle rustlers. In March they had carted away whole fields of cattle and half a dozen horses from a village just five miles away.

Lisa was standing and screaming, 'Jigsaw, Jigsaw, where are you?'

Paul said, 'That won't do any good, stoopid. They're taken away, gone, dead.' He looked frozen to where he stood.

'Let's look outside,' said Ben. 'Come on, standing won't get us anywhere.'

There were hoofmarks across the common.

'So some of them got away,' he said.

Everyone was in the yard now, except for Mary and, of course, Dad, who had gone to work hours ago.

'I'll ring the police,' James said.

'I'm going to be sick,' Paul said. 'My father will sue you for this. Apollo cost a thousand pounds. You didn't shut his door.'

Mummy and Mrs Mills took him inside. Ben found his bike. Mine had a puncture, so I ran across the common on foot with Lisa just behind me. There were plenty of hoofmarks on the common, but whether they were last night's or yesterday's or from the day before we didn't know.

Ben shouted, 'I'm doing a broad sweep. See you in half an hour.'

I walked on, imagining the ponies dead already, stripped of their skins, meat for dogs or humans. I could feel tears coming now, an endless, stupid flow.

Lisa took my hand. 'Poor little Jigsaw,' she said. 'Poor darling Jigsaw.'

'He may not be dead. We mustn't give up hope,' I said.

The sky was clearing, but it was still a dank, dreary day. We are doomed, I thought. I felt it last night. Why didn't I stay up?

Ben looked mad, bicycling through the village in his Paisley dressing gown. The church clock struck eight.

'We've forgotten halters. We can't do much if we do find them. We had better go home and get dressed properly; perhaps the police know something, perhaps they've found them,' I said, without much hope.

'This is the third thing. First we didn't sell the house, then Mary came and now the ponies have gone,' Lisa said. She was wearing trousers, and plimsolls which were soaked through and an old grey jersey which had once been mine.

'Some of them got away. Ben saw the hoofmarks,' I said.

'But where are they, then?' cried Lisa.

'In a lovely field eating lovely grass,' I replied quickly but without conviction.

'I can just imagine some awful woman wearing Jigsaw's coat,' said Lisa when we reached the yard again. 'His lovely piebald coat.'

Ben was coming back. 'Old Mr Baker thinks he heard hoofs in the night. He said a stranger rode through the village,' he cried.

'You know he's dotty,' I answered. 'What strange rider any-way? It's obvious what happened. There was a cattle truck parked outside. Can't you see? They drove the ponies into it. All of them. It's as plain as plain. They've been taken away for their skins and their flesh and poor hoofs and . . .' I could go no further. I was thinking that I would never see Lorraine again, never, never. I was remembering the wonderful hours I had spent on Limpet – my first rosette, my first cup. And now Ben was crying too and I hadn't seen him do that for years. He looked too big and silly and pitiful all at once.

'We are going to find them,' he said. 'And if I do I shall shoot the men, all of them.'

We looked the other way when we passed the empty field and Apollo's box. The yard seemed quiet, empty, impossibly lonely. We found Mummy cooking breakfast in the kitchen. 'Paul won't eat a thing,' she said. 'He keeps being sick. He's back in bed. Mrs Mills is sitting with him.'

'Thank God for Mrs Mills,' replied Ben, sniffing.

'The police have all the details,' said James, tall and business-like. 'I'll go out in the Land Rover in a minute. I don't care if I am only a learner or about to be. I can still drive it.'

'No you can't,' Mummy said.

Georgie and Phillipa sat without speaking, their little monkey faces looking pinched with worry. I thought, they're not having much of a stay – we ought to do something for them, but how can we?

I didn't want any breakfast, but Mummy made me eat a bowl

of cereal. Then I rushed upstairs and took off my pyjamas and dressed properly and all the time I was thinking, it can't be true. They can't all be gone. Life can't be that awful. Sooner or later they must come back, wandering into the yard, looking hopefully into empty buckets, whinnying when they see us. It just can't be the end of Lorraine for ever and ever. I haven't jumped her in a ring yet. She hasn't won anything. She was going so well. I had such plans . . .

Ben met me in the passage. 'The police will never find them. I'm going out on my bike,' he said. 'I'll take the halters and some string. You can have the head-collars.'

'You can't lead all of them,' I answered.

'They won't all be there,' he said.

'What about Apollo? What about Paul?' I asked. 'What about him suing us?'

'Forget it. James is ringing up the horse abattoirs at Bristol and Abergavenny. There's Reading market tomorrow, so he's on to them too. He's being marvellous. Mummy's been on to Dad. Keep hoping. We will beat the swines yet,' Ben said.

I could hear Paul sobbing as I went downstairs.

Lisa was talking to Phillipa and Georgie. She had been told to amuse them, but she couldn't stop crying. James was on the telephone again.

Mrs Mills was making beds.

Mummy said, 'I suppose Mary doesn't want any breakfast again. Really, she'll wither away if she doesn't eat more. Do you think you can wake her up, Harriet? It's half past nine.'

I went back upstairs and knocked on her door. I waited, listened, knocked again.

'She isn't there,' said Mrs Mills, scurrying along the passage with a dustpan in her hand just like a little Miss Tittlemouse. 'I've done all the rooms. I've made her bed. You look for yourself.'

I didn't look. I rushed downstairs shouting, 'Mummy, Mary's gone! She's run away or something. Gone where she wasn't meant to go.'

Mummy looked as though she couldn't take any more. She said, 'I wish your father was here. I wish he wasn't at the factory. What are we going to do?'

Ben stared at us with his mouth open. 'She could have let the ponies out, just for spite,' he said. 'And stolen the others. She's capable of it.'

'She can't be,' Mummy answered quickly. 'I shall have to telephone her mother. Where did I put the number?'

'Goodness knows!'

'We had better go on looking anyway,' said Ben. 'There's no point in standing here – it's raining.'

'I'll search the woods,' I said.

'I'll meet you on the far side by the Dog and Duck. Okay?' Ben asked.

Lisa wanted to come. 'You can't lead five ponies,' she cried. 'You'll need me.'

'We'll come too,' said Georgie.

'No,' shouted Mummy. 'I don't want anyone else disappearing. Harriet must go alone. Do you hear?'

I put lots of 2p pieces in my pocket for telephone calls, and a penknife and some string and bits of bread and pony nuts. I put three head-collars round my neck. Ben had already left with a bucket over his handlebars, a map, and our three hemp halters plus string. It was still raining. One of my boots had a hole and my anorak was too small and wouldn't zip up, but otherwise I was all right.

I went through the village first and an old man called, 'Found them yet?' And I shouted, 'No.'

And he said, 'They'll be in tins of dog meat by now, you'll see,' which made me start crying again. Then I remembered Mary. 'We've lost a guest, too,' I shouted. 'A tall girl with long hair.'

'Well I never,' he said.

Then I noticed that Ben's sign had been chopped in half and I thought, I don't want to go on with the Inn if the ponies have gone for ever, because we'll never be able to afford new ones.

It was a long way to the woods down a farm track deep in mud which oozed through the hole in my boots and clung to my socks.

Heifers stared at me with large, wondering eyes. I looked for hoofmarks and found plenty, but whether they belonged to our ponies or not, I didn't know. I started to run and to call the ponies by name each in turn, but without hope. The woods were damp and dark when I reached them. There were tracks leading in all directions. I took the one on the left which led to a clearing where apple trees grew and there were ant hills lying like sand castles in the wiry grass. It was very quiet, with no sound but the rain falling through the trees. I was soaked through by this time and the head-collars had left greasy marks round my neck. I walked on thinking about Mary, wondering where she was now and when she had left and why. She hated us and we were horrid back, I thought. We should have been nice. We should have turned the other cheek but we didn't, and now we are being paid back.

I started to run again. The woods were full of fungi now and new damp primroses. I ran and ran until I could see light ahead and knew I had reached the wheat fields beyond the wood. Miraculously the sun was shining on the new green wheat and there was a rainbow in the sky. And then I saw our ponies grazing in the distance on the headland. And I started to shout 'Found! Found!' and to leap in the air with unbelievable joy. Then I was running again, my feet leaving footmarks in the new wheat, my spirits soaring.

They raised their heads and looked at me and I thought, Jigsaw's coat will never be worn by some fat lady bedecked with jewels, and we'll ride again and I started to sing, all sorts of crazy pop songs.

There were no hoofmarks on the wheat the way I walked, but when Solitaire saw me he started to trot in a circle, round and round, leaving deep hoofmarks with his large cob feet. Lorraine whinnied and walked towards me, while Limpet watched, his dark eyes alert, his black coat shining wet like patent leather.

Then I realized with a sickening leap of my stomach that Apollo wasn't there.

I unwound the head-collars from around my neck and wished that the Dog and Duck was nearer and started to wonder how I was to get the four ponies home. Everything was very still and green and the rain had stopped completely. I could hear a pigeon cooing in an elm tree. I made a halter for Limpet out of string and tied him to a tree, then I caught Lorraine and Jigsaw. Solitaire was still trotting his wheat-destroying circles, wanting me to follow him as he always did, proving his point that *he* would decide at which moment he should be caught, not me. I heard a tractor in the distance and wondered whether it would come our way and the driver see the trampled wheat. I thought of Mary lost and Apollo probably in a knacker's yard by now, and Paul crying his eyes out at home. I thought how pleased Lisa would be to see Jigsaw again and how awful it would be for Paul. Then Solitaire came up to me and announced that he was ready to be caught.

I tied Limpet and Jigsaw together and prayed that they would behave, then I vaulted on to Lorraine and, leading Solitaire on the other side, started riding along the headland of the wheat field.

It wasn't easy because there just wasn't room for four horses on the headland and, whatever I did, Solitaire's great hoofs churned up the wheat. I wondered how I would manage when I reached the road, and whether the ponies had eaten anything they shouldn't and would die of colic or poisoning.

My moment of triumph suddenly vanished, and as I rode I started to shout, 'Ben, I've got them, got them, got them,' until all my words became jumbled together. I reached a gap into the road and now I knew the way home.

The ponies pricked their ears and hurried. Jigsaw and Limpet pulled. Solitaire dragged. Cars hooted. The sun came out. Then I saw Ben coming down the road pedalling his crappy old bike as though his life depended on it.

'Gosh, well done!' he yelled, before he saw that Apollo was missing. He got off his bike then and stood waiting for me. 'I'll leave it in the hedge,' he said, flinging it down. 'We can come back later for it in the Land Rover.'

'Aren't you pleased?' I asked.

'Yes, but where's Apollo?'

'Search me.'

He took Solitaire and untied Limpet. 'Can you manage him in a head-collar?' I asked.

'I'll have to,' he said.

We were both worried about Apollo. I dreaded meeting Paul. 'Perhaps the police have found him,' I said at last.

'And perhaps they haven't,' replied Ben.

We rode through the village and the old man shouted, 'Well done!'

'If only Mary hadn't gone as well,' said Ben.

We started to trot. I thought, there may be news, we may find Apollo returned, standing in his loose-box unscathed. Mary may be back with her mother by now. Everything may be all right.

'I could cry over my sign,' said Ben. 'It took me ages to make it.'

'Mary must have chopped it up,' I answered.

'And let out all the ponies too,' Ben cried.

'Yes, out of spite,' I said. 'But what about Apollo?'

'I don't know. It doesn't fit.'

'Nor do the tyre marks if it was Mary.'

The yard was empty when we reached it. We turned out the ponies. Apollo's empty box reproached us.

'Everything's too quiet,' said Ben ominously as we walked towards the house.

Five
A long ride

Everybody was standing in the kitchen.

'We've got the ponies,' I said.

And they all started to shout, 'Hurray! Well done!'

I wanted to say, 'Except Apollo,' but Lisa wouldn't stop shouting and leaping over chairs and generally making a fool of herself.

'Except for Apollo,' yelled Ben. 'We must go on looking for him. We are not giving up.'

'I want to look too,' said Paul, with his eyes full of tears. 'I thought you had found him . . . I thought . . .' but he couldn't go on. He ran from the room in floods of tears.

'Why not Apollo?' asked Mummy.

'I don't know. That's the mystery,' Ben answered.

'Somebody look after Paul,' Mummy said.

Mrs Mills went. I wondered how we would ever manage without her. She was the kindest, nicest, most unselfish old lady I had ever met.

Mummy put the kettle on. I could smell lunch cooking in the oven. Life was going on, as usual. Then the telephone rang.

'That will be Mary's mother,' Mummy said.

'We haven't told the police yet about Mary,' James explained. 'We don't want to start an official search, unless it's absolutely necessary.' He paused. 'Where were the ponies?'

I started to explain, then Mummy came back. 'She's furious. She's going to stop all her cheques and sue us. Isn't life awful?' she said. 'She's going to try Mary's boy friend and ring back. She says she's thoroughly upset and humiliated. She sounds a thoroughly neurotic woman,' continued Mummy.

Lisa had disappeared with Georgie and Phillipa to see the ponies. Paul was still upstairs with Mrs Mills. Mummy handed us each a mug of coffee.

'What about Apollo?' I asked.

'We had better go on looking for him. He may have got separated from the others somehow,' Ben suggested. 'We can go out on the ponies now.'

'There goes the telephone again.' Mummy ran through into the hall. I looked at the electric clock above the cooker in the kitchen and saw that it was nearly one o'clock.

'Mary isn't with her boy friend,' said Mummy returning. 'Mrs Harris is coming to conduct the search herself. She doesn't want the police informed. She wants us to look for a note.'

'Mrs Mills swept up her room, any note is probably in the dustbin now,' I said.

'Oh no! Come on, we had better have lunch,' said Mummy. 'Call everybody. We can't think properly on empty stomachs.'

It was a dismal meal. Paul hardly ate a thing and Lisa was convinced that Jigsaw had colic. Mrs Mills kept on and on about there being no note in Mary's bedroom. 'I wouldn't have swept it up. I'm very careful. I am really,' she said half a dozen times.

Phillipa and Georgie remained silent too.

'I guess he's dead,' said Paul suddenly. 'Either run down by a lorry or slaughtered.'

Mummy put her arm round him. 'Don't despair,' she said. 'We will find him, I promise.'

'We are going to look for him now. We don't want any pudding. Come on, Harriet,' cried Ben.

I couldn't bear to look at Paul's face any longer. I know what it's like to love a horse. I couldn't blame him for crying even though he was ten and boys aren't supposed to cry as much as girls.

'Poor devil,' said Ben as we ran towards the stables. We found Jigsaw rolling. We stood and stared in dismay.

'Not that!' cried Ben. 'Oh no, get a head-collar, for God's sake.'

'Lisa was right,' I shouted. 'She's no fool after all.' I grabbed a head-collar and thrust it over Jigsaw's ears. Ben slapped his quarters. I hauled. He stood up shaking and sweating.

'He must have eaten lots of the wheat,' I said.

'Or something worse. Can you hold him while I telephone the vet?' asked Ben.

'All right.'

'I'll send Lisa to help.' But Lisa didn't need sending. She was there already, saying, 'I told you so. He's probably twisted his guts by now.'

I got him into Apollo's box. It was a struggle to keep him on his feet. Supposing they all have it, I thought, and I remembered that the vet's bill was one which had been coming in in red for many months.

'I got him on the radio-telephone. He's on his way,' said Ben returning. 'I'll catch the others and tack them up. Lisa can manage once he's here, can't you, Lisa?'

'I don't know,' moaned Lisa.

'You will have to. You're nine now. You're not a baby any more,' said Ben, brushing Solitaire.

'I will help her,' said Mrs Mills, appearing suddenly from no-where. 'Don't worry yourselves. I used to hunt once, side-saddle of course. I know about horses, though we had grooms in those days. Give me the halter rope, Lisa, and let your brother and sister go in search of Paul's pony. He could be hung up some-where, and it will be dark soon, and just look at the sky – there's acres of rain in it.'

'Thanks a million,' said Ben gratefully.

I caught Lorraine and tacked her up. Jigsaw was a bit calmer and Limpet looked all right. I could hear a car coming along the road now.

'Perhaps Apollo has gone back to where he came from,' suggested Mrs Mills. 'Horses do sometimes. They get homesick. Shall I ask Paul where he lived before and get James to telephone for me?'

I shouted, 'Yes,' nodding at the same time for fear she wouldn't hear. She's no fool, I thought. I wish she was our real grannie and could live here for ever.

Our vet, Roy Smart, is fortyish and not smart at all, and usually wears old jeans with gum boots turned down at the top and a riding mackintosh. Today he didn't waste any time but said at once, 'Which one is it? How long has he been like this? And what's he been eating?'

'He's been out in the woods,' I said.

'And on new wheat,' added Ben.

'He's as tight as a drum,' said Roy, feeling Jigsaw's stomach.

'You two had better go,' said Mrs Mills, 'or it will be dark before you get back. Lisa and I can manage, can't we, Lisa?'

Lisa nodded. 'Mrs Mills is one of our guests, Roy,' Ben explained, sounding a bit embarrassed. 'She's a wizard at everything.'

Mrs Mills was wearing a woolly cap, an old skirt, thick stockings, lace-up shoes, a cardigan and, over the top of it all, a pinny.

Roy bent down to shake her hand. 'I shall need a bucket of warm water and some soap,' he began. 'What about the others, are they all right?'

'We hope so,' replied Ben, mounting.

'We've had enough tragedy for one day,' I said.

'How's that?'

'It's a long story – ponies out, guests lost – we must go,' said Ben, looking at the sky.

Lisa had gone to the house for water and soap. Mrs Mills was still holding Jigsaw when we left. He lifted his head and whinnied and then whirled round and round, but Mrs Mills held on, looking small, tough and indomitable. I hoped that I would be like her when I was eighty.

The church clock struck two, the common was misty and empty and glistening wet. Our ponies were tired from their night out; we were tired too.

'Let's go a different way this time,' suggested Ben.

'We are looking for Apollo, okay?' I asked.

'Yes, that's right. Mary's probably in London by now, lost for ever,' replied Ben.

'Is James going for your bike?' I asked.

'I forgot to tell him about it,' replied Ben.

We were cantering now. We each had a head-collar round our waist and pockets full of pony nuts.

'Mummy's going to ring Paul's parents later. She has booked a call to Washington,' Ben said.

'That will cost a pretty penny, and supposing everything gets in the papers?' I asked.

'We're finished then,' replied Ben.

'If only we knew the answers,' I said. 'Why Mary went? Who let the horses out and why? Nothing makes much sense, does it?'

'There must be an answer. It's probably quite simple really,' Ben replied.

We rode down a long stony lane and into a dark wood of conifers. We stopped to look for hoofmarks. We called, 'Anyone about?'

The trees were close together and the wood was dark and wet. We were both glad when we reached the other side. We rode up a chalky hill which smelt of thyme. We stood at the top and stared across three counties and saw trains and small neat farms, and great round nuclear towers looking as though they were built out of sand, and a village with a church, and cows looking like toy animals in the distance. But no Apollo.

'We should have brought Dad's binoculars,' Ben said.

We rode down the other side, our ponies slipping on the chalky ground, and now we could see a motorway weaving like a snake through the hills. Lorraine neighed and we stopped and stared until our eyes ached, but there was no answering neigh, only rabbits fleeing to their burrows at our approach, and the same wonderful smell of herbs and wild grasses.

There was a huge bridge sweeping across the motorway looking proud and alien and lonely.

We halted and sat hating it for slicing across the valley and the motorway for cutting the valley in half.

'If Apollo got on to the motorway, he's dead, because you don't think any of those speed merchants could or would stop for a pony, do you?' asked Ben with hate in his voice.

'No I don't, but if there was a crash surely there would be some sign of it?' I asked.

Ben shook his head. 'No, it would have been swept up clean and forgotten ages ago – just another accident, don't you know!'

'But the police would know. Someone would have mentioned a horse,' I replied.

We couldn't cross the motorway except by the terrifying bridge. 'He wouldn't have crossed that anyway,' said Ben, turning Solitaire. 'Let's go through Hangars Wood and on to Wadlington and back over Chalk Hill.'

'And back through the woods where I found the others?'

Ben nodded. We rode down a grassy track which had once been a railway line. I imagined all the people who had gone along it for fifty years or more in a little train pulled by a steam engine, clutching their suitcases or shopping bags – old ladies, children, men on their way to work. We passed the remains of a station. A young couple were living in the waiting-room. Garden tools were kept in the ticket office. We stopped and called, 'Seen a pony?'

They came out on to the track and said, 'What sort of pony? There was one came past a couple of hours ago.' And our hopes rose.

'A chestnut?' cried Ben.

'That's right. With a girl in plaits riding it. Is that the one?' The woman was clutching a baby. The man had an haversack over one shoulder and looked like an artist. We shook our heads and rode on.

Wadlington was full of shoppers. The bank was shut. We stopped and asked people if they had seen a loose pony. They looked at us as though we were mad.

'What, in the town?' they asked.

'Yes.' Ben even went into the post office to ask. Then he remembered the riding school on the other side.

'We had better try there,' he said. 'It's only half a mile further on.' So we clattered through the town, Lorraine shying at the pedestrian crossing. And someone shouted, 'Ride him, cowboy!'

Solitaire slipped and slid and nearly fell. Then we were on the other side of the town riding down a quiet road.

'It's getting late,' Ben said. 'We had better hurry.'

The riding school had thirty ponies. It was run by an elderly lady called Miss Jackson. She had given us our first riding lessons. She was old and weather-beaten and charged too little for her lessons. She drove an old car and people laughed at her, but I think she was happy.

We found her cleaning tack. We dismounted to rest our ponies and Ben told her in great detail what had happened. Once he had been devoted to her. It had been, 'Well, Miss Jackson says this,' and, 'Miss Jackson says that,' until Mummy had screamed, 'If you say "Miss Jackson" again, I shall go mad.'

Today she looked even older, but she was just as nice and kind as usual.

'I should try the abbatoirs,' she said when Ben stopped talking. 'There's one at Bristol and one at Abergavenny.'

'We have,' I said.

'And why would the thieves leave the others?' asked Ben.

'Perhaps they got away. Or perhaps they only had room for one, or perhaps they were disturbed,' suggested Miss Jackson.

'But there's much more flesh on Solitaire,' argued Ben.

'Perhaps he's difficult to catch and box.'

'Yes he is, you're dead right,' said Ben.

'And Lorraine hates men,' I said.

'And Jigsaw and Limpet are small and both still a bit thin,' suggested Ben.

Some children were filling up buckets and everything smelt

wonderful, a glorious mixture of saddle soap, horse dung and hay. I wished we could stay. But Ben was already mounting, saying, 'Well goodbye then, and thank you very much.'

'I will ring you up if I hear or see anything,' promised Miss Jackson. 'You have told the police, haven't you?'

Ben nodded. Lorraine snatched at her reins and jogged. The children filling buckets stopped to stare at us.

'Coming here makes me feel old,' exclaimed Ben.

It was ten miles home. 'I wonder how Limpet is,' I said.

'Do you think Mrs Harris will have arrived yet?' Ben asked.

'I expect so.'

'Poor Mummy!'

'I expect Dad will be home by now.'

The shops were shutting in Wadlington. The motorway was crowded with cars looking like toy cars in the distance, racing, jockeying for position. The railway track was quiet and peaceful. The young couple waved to us from the waiting-room and called, 'Any luck?'

We shook our heads and I was suddenly filled with a sense of doom. Everything is going wrong – Mary has gone, Paul is in tears, Apollo is lost, probably dead. I thought, we've failed everybody.

Our ponies were tired and there was evening in the air already, a damp, cloudy evening to match our spirits. There were rabbits on Chalk Hill, hiding behind bushes, and a few sheep.

'What Miss Jackson said made sense, didn't it?' asked Ben. 'The thieves could have taken Apollo and let the others out, either on purpose or by mistake.'

'But what about Mary?'

'That could be pure coincidence. After all, she was hating us all evening, and there was thunder in the air and that always makes temperamental people worse,' replied Ben.

'So she walked away in her nightie?'

'Nobody has thought of looking at her clothes, have they? So we don't know what she took,' Ben answered.

'No. Nor did we look in the larder to see what food she may have taken,' I said.

'She could have hitched and been murdered,' said Ben in a worried voice, starting to trot. 'You know – strangled by some awful man.'

We hadn't thought of that before. I started to feel sick. Neither of us spoke again for some time.

'She was just an unhappy person,' said Ben at last. 'And wouldn't you be with her mother?'

'I don't know. She was probably awful to her mother too,' I answered.

Suddenly I didn't want to get home, to face our exhausted parents and Paul and Mrs Harris. I felt like riding for ever. I wanted peace and there wasn't any anywhere.

We could see the woods now which I had run through in the morning. It seemed an age away already.

'I don't want to go home,' I said.

'Nor I,' said Ben. 'But we have to. We can't run away.'

'Paul's parents will make us pay a thousand pounds for Apollo,' I said. 'And Mary's parents will sue us for losing their daughter.'

'They can't,' Ben said.

'Mummy accepted five pounds a week extra for extra care, don't you remember?' I asked. 'Isn't that legally binding?'

'It could be, but I doubt it.'

I thought of Mummy, of how we had meant to help our parents, of how we had thought we would make a lot of money. We have been very naïve, I decided. Very gullible.

'Mrs Mills, Phillipa and Georgie are a success so far, aren't they?' asked Ben.

'They may be.'

'Let's face it, our parents haven't good business heads,' said Ben.

'Dad had once.'

We had reached the beech woods now, where some trees grew

straight and splendid while others were crowded and twisted with trying to reach the sunlight. It was nearly dark in the woods and rain started to fall, damping our already damp spirits still further.

We've wasted hours and hours and achieved nothing, I thought, as we started to canter along a track winding between trees.

The ponies knew they were going home – they lengthened their strides and fairly flew. The rain was in our faces. In places the track was deep in mud, but we were past caring about our ponies' legs; all we wanted now was to reach home as soon as possible and learn the worst. And then suddenly Ben stopped.

'Listen. I heard something,' he said. 'Someone calling.'

For a long time all we could hear was the rain falling through the trees and the creak of our saddles and Lorraine restlessly chewing her bit.

Ben kept saying, 'Shush, will you. Listen, for God's sake.'

And Lorraine turned round and round, longing to get home. And then we heard a faint call. It could have been 'Hi' or 'Help' or just someone calling their dog, but suddenly we were both filled with indescribable hope.

Ben shouted. 'It came from over there. Come on!' And then we were hurtling through the woods like maniacs, praying and laughing at the same time, having no idea of what we expected to find, but filled with hope just the same.

Six
'Why didn't you get help?'

For a time we seemed to be riding in circles. We stopped to listen, but there were no more cries for help, just the dripping trees and the approaching darkness.

'We imagined it,' I said, drawing rein. 'You know how easy it is to imagine things you want to hear, like hoof beats on the road, or the back door opening and Mummy home, when she isn't at all.'

'It wasn't imagination,' replied Ben firmly. 'It was someone calling.'

'But whom?'

'I don't know.'

We were both wet by this time and our ponies were covered with mud and sweat.

'I want to hear how Jigsaw is. It seems years since we left home,' I said.

'Let's try calling,' suggested Ben and he started to shout, 'Where are you? It's Ben.' His voice echoed and came back.

'Why should they know who Ben is?' I asked.

'Shut up,' he said. 'Just listen!' We listened and listened.

'Let's go back via the Dog and Duck,' said Ben finally. 'I know it's longer, but we haven't been that way yet today.'

'Today, is it still today?' I asked, turning a reluctant Lorraine away from the track which led straight home. I knew how she felt, we had been riding hard for five hours and now we were asking her to go somewhere else. She kept stopping and trying to go back. She must have thought we were lost or mad. Wet branches brushed against us making us wetter than we were

already; water trickled down our necks. In the distance we could see where the woods ended by the light coming through the trees. Few people walked or rode this way and the path was narrow and winding. Once we saw some deer and there were birds everywhere, settling in the trees for the night. And then suddenly our ponies stopped, their heads raised, their ears pricked.

'There's something ahead. Can you see anything?' shouted Ben.

I was leading. I could feel Lorraine trembling with excitement. Then she whinnied and went on with Solitaire snorting behind. And then we saw what we had been looking for all day long – Apollo lying on his side among the trees – and Ben said, 'Oh God, he's dead.'

'He can't be. Why? How?' I said.

The ponies stood and looked and snorted. 'Here, hold them,' shouted Ben. 'There's someone else.' We slid to the ground. I held the ponies and was glad that Ben had come, that I wasn't alone in the woods trying to cope. He ran forward. I tied the ponies to trees with string, forgetting the head-collars we carried, and went after him.

'It's Mary,' he said.

She was sitting up now. Her hair lay wet across her face.

'I've been calling,' she said in a vague voice. 'Calling and calling.'

'You've killed Apollo. He's dead,' shouted Ben. 'Dead!'

I had never seen a dead horse before. I started to shake all over.

'And you let the others out,' I yelled. 'You pig, you swine!'

She tried to speak again, but we wouldn't listen, for suddenly we were overcome with uncontrollable rage. Ben kept shouting, 'He's dead, and what will Paul do? He loved him. Can't you understand? No, of course not, you wouldn't, would you?'

'You might have killed ours, too,' I shouted. 'Jigsaw is ill with colic because of you.'

'You aren't fit to live,' yelled Ben.

'No wonder you need extra care. You'll start killing children next,' I shouted. And then, as suddenly as we shouted, our tempers evaporated. We looked at Mary and saw that she was crying silently, like someone who has reached the end of a long road and can't go any further.

'How did he die? Why didn't you get help?' asked Ben.

I saw now that Apollo was wearing his tack, and that his reins were broken and his saddle crushed.

'He's lying on my leg. It's broken,' said Mary in a whisper. She was shivering and even in the dusk I could see that there was no colour in her face. And now I was concerned for her. She might die, her neck could be broken, her back, anything. I had learned some first-aid years ago in the Brownies. I put my coat over her.

'I'll get some wood and lever poor Apollo off,' Ben said.

Solitaire was leaping about and in another second he had broken his string and was gone. 'Oh no!' I shrieked.

'It can't be helped,' said Ben, coming back with a branch. 'Just hang on to Lorraine.'

Mary was groaning now. 'I want to die,' she moaned. 'I don't want to go on any more. Please God, help me to die.'

Ben wiped his brow with the back of his hand. Lorraine neighed.

The first piece of wood was rotten and broken. Lorraine was whirling round and round by this time. And, in the gathering darkness, the wood was full of eerie sounds, strange rustles and great menacing trees. I found myself praying, 'God, make everything all right. God, make Mary live and Paul not too upset. Please, God.'

Ben swore and tried to break a young sapling. Apollo seemed very still and Mary was quite silent now, so that she could have been dead, too.

'Why don't you help?' Ben shouted at me.

'How?'

'By pulling this,' he shouted.

He was uprooting a young tree, struggling and pulling, with sweat running down his face and his hands scratched and bleeding. I seized the tree lower down and pulled, too; then something snapped and we both fell back on to soft earth. Ben was up first.

'Come on,' he shouted. 'I can't do it on my own. You will have to help.'

'I can't touch Apollo – he's dead,' I said.

'We know that. But you can help lever him off Mary's leg, can't you? Or do you want her to die?' he asked.

'I think we should go for help,' I said. 'It's too much for us. Injured people should never be moved except by experts – doctors or ambulance men, or trained nurses.'

But Ben wouldn't listen. He wedged the broken sapling under

poor dead Apollo and Mary opened her eyes and asked, 'What's happening?'

'Get ready to move,' yelled Ben in reply. 'Come on, Harriet, pull, will you, pull!'

I dug my feet into the soft, peaty earth and thought of Mummy waiting at home, wondering where we were.

The sapling bent because it was young and green. 'Hold it,' yelled Ben. 'Hold it still.'

'I can't,' I screamed, straining and pulling, feeling the wood slipping through my hands.

But Ben was on the ground now, pushing Apollo off Mary, saying, 'Pull back. What's the matter? Is your leg broken?'

Then the sapling sprang back like a catapult and we were back where we were, with Mary moaning and the darkness descending above the tree tops.

'Let's go for help,' I suggested. 'We need strong men.'

'We'll try again, we'll get it further under this time. Ready, Mary?' asked Ben.

'I want to stay here,' she answered. 'I don't want to begin again.'

'Begin what?' I asked.

'Don't listen, she's delirious,' shouted Ben.

She started to moan. It was a strange, animal sound, not human at all.

'We need a doctor and an ambulance. Please, Ben,' I pleaded. 'I can go for them on Lorraine. You can stay with Mary.'

'I won't give in. It's only her leg. She can move her back,' argued Ben. 'It's not broken.'

His face was set and determined. I had never seen him like this before. It was as though he had suddenly grown up and become a man.

We set to work again without speaking and this time we both felt Apollo shift. Then Mary gave another long moan and suddenly she was standing up, saying, 'My leg doesn't work. It's numb. I can't feel my toes at all. I can't feel anything.'

Ben put an arm round her. He was still panting from his exertions. 'You're going to be all right,' he said.

Mary looked ghastly, worse than I had ever seen anyone look before.

'How long have you been here?' I asked.

'Since last night. Or is it another day?'

'Almost,' I answered.

She was wearing trousers and a pullover on top of pink pyjamas; and wellington boots.

We heaved her on to Lorraine. Ben gave me his coat. It was still raining. I led Lorraine, while Ben held Mary in position. She was very quiet, too quiet. She looked in agony.

'Your mother is probably waiting for you at our place. You'll be all right,' I said.

'I didn't let them out,' she said, through chattering teeth. 'I swear to God.'

'But you stole Apollo. He was worth a thousand pounds. We'll have to pay compensation. We'll be ruined. And no one will come to The Black Pony Inn any more. The whole idea is finished,' said Ben bitterly.

We waited for an answer but she had drifted into sleep or unconsciousness, we didn't know which.

Ben and I didn't talk any more, because suddenly everything seemed too bad for words. I wondered how we would tell Paul that Apollo was dead, and about his parents and what they would say. I prayed that Solitaire had reached home safely. And I wondered whether Mrs Harris was in the kitchen yet, yelling at Mummy.

I wished we hadn't shouted at Mary and called her names. Dad says that you should never judge anyone until you've heard all the facts, but we had judged Mary without hesitation and said things she would never forget. I felt very tired suddenly, but in the distance we could see lights now, the lights of the village and home.

'Our parents must be beside themselves with worry,' Ben said. 'They've probably sent out a search party for us.'

'At least we've got Mary,' I replied.

'We will have to send the horse slaughterers for Apollo,' Ben said.

'Why did he die?'

'We'll soon know. She'll have to explain,' Ben said.

The village was wet and silent. Lights shone out from cottage windows. A dog barked. The common was empty.

We found Solitaire in the yard, his reins broken. Jigsaw was still in Apollo's box. We left Solitaire as he was and led Lorraine to the house. Then Ben yelled, 'Open the door. We've got Mary. Open up.' And Mummy came out, looking all in pieces, followed by Dad.

'She's unconscious,' Ben said.

'Telephone for a doctor,' shouted Dad, picking her up in his arms. Mummy ran back indoors. Mrs Mills looked out of a window. 'I'll put some hot-water bottles in her bed,' she called.

I stood holding Lorraine, feeling numb, exhausted inside and out, while Ben ran back to the yard to see to Solitaire. Presently I put Lorraine in a box and bedded her down. I didn't want to go inside and run into Paul. I didn't want to explain. Ben put Solitaire in another loose-box. We rubbed them down and left them with water and feeds and their rugs inside out with straw under them. I felt stiff all over.

'We had better go in, we can't stay out here for ever,' Ben said.

We put our tack in the tack-room. It looked sodden and broken and I remembered Paul's tack lying in the wood with Apollo.

'We had better go in and explain,' Ben said.

I followed him up to the house, my feet squelching inside my wet boots.

Seven
'I just love that horse'

James was sitting in the kitchen with his head in his hands.

'Paul has gone. Mrs Mills thinks he was kidnapped,' he said.

'Gone?' I cried. 'Him too?'

Ben collapsed into a chair. 'No. It's impossible. It's like ten green bottles hanging on the wall. You know the song,' he said, trying to laugh, trying to make us all laugh, but failing utterly.

'We were out,' continued James, raising his head to look at us. 'Mrs Mills was with Georgie and Phillipa. She says she heard a car come up the drive; then someone banged on the door; but by the time she got downstairs, the car was gone and she found a note in the hall saying "I can't stay any longer" and signed "Paul". The police have the note now. Mummy tried to get his parents on the telephone, but they weren't there. It's been awful here – awful – Mummy crying, Dad shouting, Mrs Mills putting on the kettle and saying the same things over and over again, and never hearing anybody's answers.'

'We had a bad time too – Apollo's dead,' said Ben.

'Oh no, not that too!' cried James. 'How did he die?'

'We don't know yet,' Ben answered.

Mummy came into the room then. She had lines on her face I had never seen before. 'Thank God, you're back,' she said.

'Are you ready for some more bad news?' asked Ben.

'I don't know. What is it?' she asked, pushing her hair back.

'Apollo's dead,' Ben said.

'Dead!' she cried. 'But how?'

At that moment Dr Hobbs pushed open the back door, saying, 'May I come in? Where's the patient?'

'Upstairs. She looks awful,' said Mummy in a distracted voice. 'Follow me.'

He smiled at us as he rushed through the kitchen clutching a bag. 'Cheer up,' he said. 'Every cloud has a silver lining.'

'Our clouds grow blacker every moment,' I muttered.

'You've said it,' agreed Ben.

James handed us mugs of steaming coffee. My mug had been a special offer on a brand of coffee. It had Princess Anne and Mark Phillips on it.

'Is Mrs Harris still coming?' Ben asked.

'Yes, she's on her way. She wasn't much perturbed by the news. There was no panic, no screams. I don't think she cares much for Mary. I think she would like her dead just as long as she could put the blame on someone else,' replied James.

'Charming,' said Ben.

'Poor Mary. But what about Jigsaw?' I asked. 'Is he all right?'

'You had better ask Lisa,' replied James.

I wondered what Dr Hobbs was doing upstairs. I hoped Mary's back wasn't broken, that she wouldn't have to go about on crutches for the rest of her life. I was very tired in spite of the coffee and when you're tired everything seems worse. I thought, supposing she never walks again, and we're sued for damages and Dad has to pay fifty thousand pounds; we'll be ruined for life.

And the clock went on ticking as though nothing had happened, ticking our lives away.

James fetched bread and cheese from the larder. 'Why did Apollo die?' he asked.

'We don't know. We expect Mary killed him and smashed her own leg in the process,' replied Ben.

'She looked awful when Dad carried her in. I thought she was dying,' James said.

'Shouldn't we be looking for Paul?' I asked, standing up ready for action.

'The police are looking. They have panda cars touring the

countryside. We are waiting for a ransom note,' replied James, making himself another mug of coffee.

'I think he's searching for Apollo,' said Lisa, coming into the kitchen. 'It was still daylight when he went and he had been crying ever since lunch. Is Apollo really dead?'

I nodded. 'Dead as a doornail,' said Ben.

She started to cry. 'It's so awful for Paul,' she said.

'How is Jigsaw?' I asked.

'Okay. We were just in time. Roy thinks he must have eaten a lot of young wheat,' she said.

We could hear Dr Hobbs coming down the stairs now. We heard him say, 'I will arrange for the ambulance to be here at ten in the morning. I've given her a sedative. If she wakes up, give her warm fluids with plenty of sugar, but nothing after 5 AM as she will probably be having an anaesthetic.'

Mummy showed him out the front way. 'Thank you for coming,' she said, shutting the door after him.

'It could be worse,' she said, coming into the kitchen. 'It's a simple fracture of the femur and she's suffering from exposure and exhaustion, but there're no complications at the moment like pneumonia or bronchitis.'

'No broken neck?' I asked.

'Of course not, silly,' replied Mummy.

'I hear a car,' cried Ben.

'That will be Mrs Harris,' said Mummy.

'Let Dad deal with her – you've had enough misery for one day,' suggested James.

'He's out looking for Paul.'

Mrs Harris rushed into the kitchen like a hurricane, leaving the back door open. 'Well, have you found her?' she cried in a high-pitched voice.

If she had been a dog she would have been yapping, with her hackles up, spoiling for a fight. It was obvious that she hadn't shed a tear for Mary, for she was perfectly made up and smelling of expensive perfume, whereas we all looked grey with fatigue

64

and Mummy hadn't a spot of make-up on her face, and was still wearing the disreputable pinny she had put on at lunchtime.

'Yes. She's upstairs with a broken leg,' Mummy replied.

'So she *is* hurt! I knew it,' said Mrs Harris.

'She's sedated. Everything is under control, the doctor's been,' continued Mummy. 'She's going into hospital in the morning. Would you like a drink?'

'No. I must see her at once. I must know what's happened,' cried Mrs Harris.

'She won't tell you, because she's asleep,' replied Mummy, leading the way upstairs.

Ben and I went outside to put our ponies' rugs the right way in. The ponies were very tired and rather cross. We topped up their water and gave them the last of the oat straw. Then we returned indoors and presently Mrs Mills, Georgie and Phillipa appeared, wanting supper, but there wasn't any prepared so James started opening tins.

'We must do something about Apollo,' said Ben. 'We can't leave him in the wood and there must be a post-mortem. I think I will ring Roy.'

His energy had come back, whereas I still felt like a damp rag. I longed to go to bed and sleep and sleep and then to wake up and find that everything was all right.

I started to lay the table, missing out Paul's and Mary's places.

James was cooking curry, which he loves. I opened a tin of mince and we found some rice and saw that James already had a saucepan of tomato soup bubbling on the cooker. 'Spoons for curry,' said James. 'Don't forget.'

I didn't agree with spoons, but I was too tired to argue.

'Mary was out all night in all that rain,' I said.

'Roy is coming here to pick me up first thing in the morning, as soon as it's light,' Ben said, returning. 'He wants us to question Mary.'

'She won't be awake by then,' I replied.

'She'll have to be.'

We ate supper too worried and too tired for conversation. It was very late. Dad was still out looking for Paul. The police hadn't telephoned, nor had Paul's parents. It was awful sitting and eating and all the time not knowing where Paul was.

'He was such a nice boy,' said Lisa, helping to clear the table.

'Was!' cried Ben. 'You're making him dead already.'

Mrs Harris had decided to stay the night. Mummy made up a bed for her in the room next to Mary's which had once been her sewing-room. Mrs Harris didn't speak a word to me or Ben. She fetched a small case from her car and disappeared upstairs.

I took Georgie and Phillipa up to bed. They said, 'Need we wash and clean our teeth?' And I said, 'No, just forget it.'

'Do you think Paul's dead?' asked Georgie.

I shook my head.

'But where is he then?'

'The police will find him. They always find people.' But I didn't believe what I said because I knew there are lots of people who are never found.

'Will they put his photograph outside police stations?' Phillipa asked.

'I don't know.'

'What will his parents do?'

'Sue us, I expect.'

'That won't find Paul. Will they send out the army?' asked Georgie.

'And drag rivers?' asked Phillipa.

'We'll see,' I replied, suddenly too weary for words, too weary for anything. They looked small and sweet in bed. I tucked them up.

'You'll soon be home,' I said. 'Have you heard from Mummy yet?'

'Yes, we got postcards. She's all right.'

I could see they wouldn't sleep. I remembered things Mummy had said to me when I was little. 'Think of something nice, think about Christmas,' I whispered, tiptoeing from the room.

It was nearly ten o'clock. 'Have a hot bath and go to bed,' Mummy told me when I appeared downstairs. 'Your father and I are taking it in turns to stay up in case the call comes through from Washington. Their time is different from ours. And the police may telephone about Paul, but you needn't stay up.'

I looked out of the passage window and everything was bathed in moonlight. I could see the ponies looking over their loose-box doors. Was Paul out there somewhere in the moonlight? Or locked up somewhere waiting for ransom money? I wondered. Ben came and stood beside me.

'I think he's lost,' he said.

'I think he's kidnapped,' I replied.

'We can't do any more now but I want you to help me tomorrow,' he said. 'You know Mary.'

'I ought to.'

'I must question her before I go out with Roy. He wants to know what happened before Apollo died. He may have eaten yew. She may have ridden him to death, or tried to kill him in a fit of madness. I'm going to set my clock. Roy plans to be here some time after six; we'll have to wake up Mary and talk to her. I need you.'

'She may not wake up whatever we do,' I said.

'I'll call you at five forty-five. Okay? We'll slap her with wet towels if necessary,' replied Ben.

'Okay.'

I went upstairs to the attics. Georgie and Phillipa were asleep, cuddling a variety of stuffed animals. The moonlight cast strange shadows across the room. I climbed into my humble iron bed. I wanted to pray for Paul, to ask God to bring him back at once, but I fell asleep before I got further than 'Please, God'. And it seemed but a minute later that Ben was shaking me by the shoulder, saying, 'Wake up. We've got to question Mary – remember?' He drew back a curtain. In the distance cocks were crowing. Outside everything was still and misty, waiting for the day to begin in earnest.

'Don't be long,' he whispered. 'There isn't much time.'

'Any news in the night?' I whispered, madly rubbing my eyes.

'I don't know yet,' he said.

'Any telephone calls?' I insisted.

'I didn't hear any, but you know me, I sleep like a log.'

He was dressed in a big sweater, corduroys and thick socks. He tiptoed from the room.

I thought, supposing she screams and wakes the whole house? Her mother is in the next room. She will go crazy. But I knew it was a risk we had to take because somehow we had to know why Apollo had died.

Phillipa stirred and muttered 'Mummy' as I put on my dressing gown which I had had since I was nine and now only reached to my knees.

Ben was waiting outside my door. He had brushed his hair.

'We must be friendly this time,' he said. 'No nasty names.'

'You called her names, too,' I answered.

'I know and I bitterly regret it,' he said. We crept down the attic stairs. 'We can't knock or her mother will hear. You go first,' whispered Ben.

Mary was lying partly curled up with one leg awkwardly alone under the blankets as though it were detached from the rest of her body. She was heavily asleep. Her hair lay sprawled across the pillow and she was snoring. I was afraid to touch her.

I said, 'Mary, wake up. It's me, Harriet.'

'Don't say your name, you know she hates us,' whispered Ben. 'Touch her, gently, don't shake her.'

'I'm not a fool,' I retorted.

I touched her shoulder and whispered, 'Mary, wake up. Please wake up.'

She wasn't cold any more and the room smelt of antiseptic. She stirred and groaned and muttered something. I shook her gently. 'What happened to Apollo?' I said. 'Please, you must tell us, it's vital, please.'

'I didn't kill him. I went after the others. He bolted. He went
mad, it was awful.' Tears ran down her cheeks.

'Isn't that enough?' I asked.

'Who let them out?' said Ben.

'I was trying to help,' she answered, opening her eyes. 'I
swear to God I was. What are you doing here anyway. Get out of
my room.'

'The vet has to know. He's doing a post-mortem,' said Ben.

Her eyes were shutting again. 'It wasn't my fault. He went
mad. He went on and on, mile after mile. Then he died,' she
muttered.

We crept from the room. The passage outside was full of sunlight.

'Do you think she's speaking the truth?' I asked.

'Yes.'

We went downstairs and made ourselves mugs of tea in the kitchen, heaping sugar into them to give us energy.

'But why did he go mad?' I asked.

'He may have had a fright and died of heart failure.'

'But he looked all right when he came.'

We drew back the curtains.

Dad appeared from the sitting-room. His clothes were crumpled. 'No call from Washington. Pour me a mug of tea, please,' he said.

'What about Paul?' I asked.

'The police brought him back. They found him wandering along the B20, completely lost,' Dad said.

'He wasn't kidnapped then?' asked Ben.

'No, Lisa was right. He was looking for Apollo. Mrs Mills must have dreamed up the car or else it was a bunch of sightseers sizing up the joint,' replied Dad.

'Did you tell Paul that Apollo was dead?' asked Ben.

'No.'

So that awful moment had still to come. 'I thought you could tell him, Harriet,' Dad said.

'Me? I can't. Ben, you're the nearest him in years. I wouldn't know how to begin,' I cried.

'Just try,' said Daddy wearily.

We heard a car horn. 'That's Roy,' Ben said, slipping out of the back door.

'I'm going back to bed,' I said. 'Thank goodness Paul came back before his parents telephoned.'

'Yes. We only have to tell them about their horse now,' Dad answered. 'Let's hope he was insured. Be gentle with Paul when you tell him, Harriet. Take him out for a ride. He can ride Jigsaw, can't he?'

'If Lisa doesn't mind, but it will be a bit of a come down after Apollo, won't it?' I asked.

I went back to bed, but I couldn't sleep and presently Phillipa and Georgie woke up and wanted to know whether Paul was back. They were pleased when I told them that he was safe asleep in bed.

'Does he know about Apollo?' Georgie asked, sitting up.

'Not yet. Please don't tell him. I'm going to tell him on a ride,' I said.

'Okay. Can we ride?'

'Yes, afterwards,' I said.

I wanted to get the awful task over with, but it was hours before Paul got up and there was still no sign of Ben; nor had the call from Washington come through.

But then at ten o'clock the ambulance came and Mrs Harris escorted the men upstairs, her lips tight and disagreeable. They carried Mary down on a stretcher, still half asleep.

'I'm going with her,' said Mrs Harris. 'I don't suppose you'll see either of us ever again. I've stopped the cheque.'

I thought, we'll never know what really happened then. How sad. And she'll never be grateful for us finding her and bringing her home. And we'll never know why she behaves as she does. It was like getting half-way through a crossword puzzle and having to stop, only much worse because it was real life. Perhaps I can write to her, I thought.

James was helping Mrs Harris with her suitcase. One of the ambulance men tucked a blanket round Mary's legs. She lay looking at the roof of the ambulance. I wanted to scream, 'What really happened? Tell us, please, so we can tell Paul.' But I knew it would only cause a scene. She was going away and I would never know her any better, or apologize for calling her names. It was life.

Paul was behind me now. He said, 'Where's Apollo? I must know.'

'He's hurt,' I answered, hating myself for lying. 'Will you come out for a ride now? I think you could do with it.'

There were dark circles under his eyes. 'Okay. I'll just get kitted out,' he said.

I felt cornered and terribly alone waiting in the yard for Paul.

71

It was a lovely morning. Everything was suddenly sparkling and the trees were still at last, basking in the sunlight. Jigsaw was sleepy. Lorraine stood with her head up looking for further adventure. It isn't fair, I thought, why should I tell him?

It wasn't a morning for bad news. It was a morning for silver cups and red rosettes and great hopes being realized.

I wondered how Ben and Roy were getting on in the wood. They had been away a long time already. Perhaps Mary had ridden Apollo into a tree, perhaps she had gone mad, not Apollo. Would we ever know the truth? I wondered.

Paul came at last, smiling. 'I hear the vet has been. Has he taken Apollo to hospital to make him better?'

'No, not really,' I answered quickly with a choke in my voice, thinking of the Horse Slaughterer's truck which had 'Horse Ambulance' written across the front when it should have had 'Death Cell' or 'Mortuary', and how it was probably in the wood by now taking away Apollo. I could feel tears running down my cheeks and I hid my face in Lorraine's mane saying, 'Are you ready to get up?'

Paul nodded.

I tightened Jigsaw's girth, and Paul said, 'You're crying, why?'

I didn't answer. I ran down his stirrups and said, 'Jigsaw is lovely to ride. Not like Apollo, but nice and kind, and very, very brisk. He trots very fast too,' but my words got mixed up with my misery and came out shaky.

'I can take bad news,' replied Paul, mounting. 'Don't worry about me. If Apollo's broken a leg, I don't mind waiting until it's mended. I don't mind waiting years. I just love that horse.'

I mounted Lorraine. Her neck in front of me gave me comfort, her pricked ears gave me courage. I'll wait a bit and then tell him after a canter, I thought. I'll break it gently, bit by bit. 'We'll go across the fields. I'm sick of the woods,' I said. 'Are you okay? Are your stirrups right?'

Paul was smiling again now. 'I remember the first time I saw

Apollo,' he began. 'I saw him, and knew he had to be mine. Has that ever happened to you?'

I shook my head. 'Lorraine was dead cheap,' I said. 'She was skin and bone in the market.'

'He'll mend, won't he? Broken legs mend nowadays?' asked Paul.

'Some,' I said. 'Shall we canter?'

Paul wasn't much of a rider. I wondered how he had ever managed Apollo. We drew rein and he said, 'Hi. Look. There's the horse ambulance. It must be bringing Apollo home. Let's go back. I want to see him.'

And my silly tears came back and I said, 'No you can't, you'll never see Apollo again. He's dead.'

But Paul didn't believe me. He said, 'Sure and no kidding,' and, 'Thanks a lot.'

I looked at him and said, 'I'm sorry. We don't know why he died. The vet is doing a post-mortem on him now. It's just one of those things.' And my tears fell into Lorraine's mane and I wished that Ben were there to explain things better than I could.

Then Paul said, 'I want to go back anyway. I want to speak to my parents back home.'

And I thought, I've made a muck of it. I make a muck of everything. And we turned round and rode back.

We found Mummy opening letters in the kitchen. 'All these people want to come and live with us, isn't it extraordinary?' she asked.

'We can't have them,' I said. 'We can't have any more. It's too awful.'

'He knows then?' asked Mummy looking at Paul, going to him, putting her arms round him.

He pushed her away and said, 'I don't want sympathy. I want to talk to my parents *now*.'

'We've been waiting for them to call since yesterday evening,' explained Mummy, 'and we're still waiting.'

'Can we ride now?' shrieked Georgie and Phillipa, coming into the kitchen. 'We've been waiting for ages.'

'Put on hard hats,' said Mummy. 'I'll look after Paul, Harriet. You've had enough misery for one day.'

'By the way, the sign's gone,' I said.

'I know. Colonel Jones chopped it down on behalf of the parish,' Mummy answered.

'Just one more blow,' I said.

'When things are better we will put up another one,' Mummy said. 'Your father's getting permission.'

'Who are we riding?' shrieked Georgie and Phillipa, charging downstairs. 'Do we need whips?'

Eight
A call from Washington

I tacked up Limpet for them. I had left Jigsaw waiting with his tack on. I took them to the smallest field by the stables which we call the paddock and I pretended we were preparing for a dressage test. I made them enter the arena at a trot and halt at X (which was a cross made out of sticks) and salute and then ride forward straight. Limpet dawdled, but Jigsaw, remembering his days in a cart, trotted straight as a die. I made them change ponies and back straight between poles on the ground, but all the time my mind was elsewhere with Ben and Roy in the dark damp wood, or with Paul, heartbroken in the house. I made them ride without stirrups and then take them back and have a walk and trot race and I wondered how Mary was in hospital and whether we would ever see her again. The sun was shining and there were flies round the ponies' heads and Phillipa and Georgie decided to take off their coats. I put up little jumps for them and a grid.

'Hold on to the mane if you feel unsteady,' I shouted. 'Not too long a run. Don't start till the pony in front is over.' And all the time I was wondering where we would live if we decided to give up the Inn. And what I would do with Lorraine. We had some more races and then an hour was up and we untacked the ponies together and turned them out, and Georgie in a rush of affection held my hand and Phillipa told me how her father always shouted at breakfast. And I said, 'Fathers always shout at breakfast. It must be almost lunchtime by now. Race you to the house,' and they rushed after me screaming and all the time I was wondering whether the call had come through from Washington and what Paul's parents had said.

Georgie and Phillipa wouldn't stop talking now. 'I suppose the Inn is named after Limpet?' asked Georgie.

'That's right,' I answered, opening the back door.

'Did you learn to ride on him?'

'Yes, that's right.'

'He's a super pony. Has he won many rosettes?' asked Georgie.

'About a hundred all told,' I said.

'What about Jigsaw?'

'We haven't had him so long. He's won about fifty.'

'You must be terribly good riders,' gasped Georgie.

'No, just lucky.'

There was no sign of anyone. I stood in the kitchen listening, praying that nothing else had gone wrong.

Then the telephone rang and I rushed through into the hall and picked up the receiver and a voice said, 'I have your personal call to Washington. Can you take it?' And I felt sick suddenly. 'Hang on,' I shrieked and rushed through the house shouting, 'It's the Washington call.'

Mummy and Paul came hurtling down the stairs together, but Paul got to the phone first. 'Is that you, Mom?' he cried. 'Something terrible's happened. Apollo's dead.'

'Hold on a minute,' said the voice at the other end, 'you're not through yet.'

'I wanted to speak first, to explain,' said Mummy.

Georgie and Phillipa disappeared in search of Lisa. The sun sent dusty shafts of light across the hall. Time seemed to stand still.

'God knows what they'll do,' said Mummy. She looked haggard. I wanted to put my arms round her and say, 'Everything's going to be all right,' but I couldn't because I didn't believe it myself. At this moment, I saw only failure ahead – the house up for sale again, being sold for next to nothing, the end of our dream.

'It's me, Paul. Is that Mom?'

We heard his father's voice loud and clear saying, 'No, it's me,

Paul, what's biting you? We've been at the cabin in the mountains.'

'It's Apollo. He's dead.'

I wanted to shut my ears but I couldn't. I tried not to listen, but I could hear the anger vibrating along the line and Mummy seemed to shrink as she listened. I wished that Ben or James or Dad were there to comfort Mummy.

'No, I don't know how he died. The girl took him – no, a house guest,' Paul said. 'Yes, stole him, stole my horse, Dad. Yes. She killed him. Rode him to death.'

I thought of the minutes passing, adding pounds to our bill. I thought, there is no end to it, no way out – he's dead, and death can't be bypassed or excused or conveniently exchanged for something, or forgotten.

I went and stood by Mummy and said, 'It will pass. Time is a great healer,' which she had said to me once a long, long time ago when I had done something idiotic and killed a friendship for ever.

'Sure. He wants to speak to you,' Paul said, holding out the receiver.

Mummy took it. 'I can't say how sorry I am,' she began but Mr Armstrong cut in on her, shouting that we weren't fit to look after guests or animals. I wanted to snatch the phone away and try to explain, to say, 'Leave Mummy out of it, it wasn't her fault.'

But now I could hear Ben shouting, 'Anyone at home?' and then, 'Do you want a cup of coffee, Roy?' And I rushed into the kitchen and Ben put his thumbs up and said, 'It's okay.' He was carrying Apollo's tack and it started me crying again.

'Mr Armstrong is on the telephone, he's shouting at Mummy,' I cried. 'He's being awful about Apollo. He says it's all her fault. It's awful.'

Roy was in his usual clothes, his boots were covered with mud and his hair had leaves in it. 'He is, is he? Well, let me speak to him,' he said.

He strode into the hall and took hold of the phone and we

heard him say, 'Excuse me, I'm a veterinary surgeon, yes, a horse doctor if you like, and I've just done a post-mortem on your pony and you're lucky he *is* dead.'

And Ben whispered, 'It's all right, Harriet. Stop crying.'

'Yes. He had a tumour. He could have gone mad with your boy on top and killed him. It was pressing on his brain. Didn't you have him vetted when you bought him? Oh I see, what a pity. I expect he was pretty quiet for such a well-bred pony, well, sleepy.'

We could hear Mr Armstrong arguing but Roy said firmly, 'I will be mailing the lab report and the results of all the tests to you during the next few days. Show them to any veterinary college in the world if you like. I can send you the tumour, too, if you want it. He really died just in time, another day and your boy would have been on top and he might be lying in hospital with a fractured skull or worse.'

'Good old Roy,' whispered Ben.

'The call will cost a fortune,' I said.

'Never mind, we're saved,' replied Ben.

'Well, I should ask the people here to choose your next pony. They're no fools and I will vet it for you personally, for nothing if you like. Yes, of course.' He handed the receiver back to Paul and I heard him say, 'Well, I like Jigsaw and I'd like to stay on as arranged as a house guest, sure I would.'

And Ben pretended to faint and Mummy said, 'Well I never. What a surprise.' Then Roy said, 'I must be off,' and Mummy shook him warmly by the hand and said, 'I can never thank you enough.' And Roy replied, 'You don't have to, it's all in a day's work.'

Ben showed him out and when he returned we saw for the first time how filthy he had become. 'Take your boots off at once!' shouted Mummy. 'Just look at my clean floor.'

But Ben only laughed, saying, 'I'm going to be a vet when I'm grown up, I've decided at last. We went to the lab at the veterinary college. I helped him all the way.'

Paul put down the receiver and said, 'Dad says I'm to tell you I'm real sorry and so is he. And I want to stay on if I may and I want Harriet to teach me to ride properly and help me buy a pony. Okay?'

'Okay,' said Ben and I together.

He held out his hand and we all shook it in turn and Mummy said, 'This calls for a drink. How about some cider?'

And Lisa came tearing downstairs shouting, 'Cider, yes please.' And James and Dad appeared five minutes later and we all sat together drinking cider. And Paul said, 'I'm real sorry about everything.' And I replied, 'It was natural. I would have felt the same if Lorraine had died.'

'I want a cute pony next time, something like Jigsaw,' he said. 'What we call an apache pony back home.'

'You'll need something of fourteen hands because you're going to grow,' advised Ben. 'Not like Lisa.'

'I'm not the smallest in my class any more, Angy is,' retorted Lisa.

We all started to feel drunk quite soon, not with drink but with relief.

There was hotpot in the oven for supper and Mrs Mills came down and had a tot of whisky with Dad. Paul was still rather quiet, but not bitter any more and after a time I found *Horse and Hound* and we read it together, searching for a suitable pony for him. 'I'll sure have it vetted this time,' he said. 'We trusted the people who sold us Apollo and they were real cheats, no kidding.'

'He must be quiet and sensible and a good jumper,' I said.

'And quiet in traffic,' added Ben.

'With a kind eye,' said Lisa.

'I don't want another chestnut. If I can't have a pinto, I would like a black,' said Paul.

'"A good horse is never a bad colour,"' quoted Ben.

'There's the telephone again,' said James.

'More disaster,' exclaimed Ben.

'We should leave it off the hook,' said Dad, going to the telephone then coming back to say, 'It's Mrs Harris, it's for you, Harriet.'

'For me?' I cried. 'It can't be. It must be Mummy she wants.'

'She said *you*,' replied Dad, sitting down again.

I went through to the hall shaking with trepidation. I thought, she's suing me for slander or something equally ghastly.

'Hullo, it's Harriet here,' I said. Then I saw that my hand was trembling which was something it had never done before.

'Mary wants to see you and Ben. She insists,' said Mrs Harris with disagreeable reluctance as though it was the most unsavoury request she had ever made.

'I thought hospitals didn't allow child visitors,' I said, to gain time to think.

'She's got round Sister,' replied Mrs Harris. 'I don't know how. Can you come?'

'What for?' I answered.

'For a chat.'

'For a chat?' I replied, unbelieving. 'Are you sure?'

'Yes. And Ben. Any time after ten o'clock in the morning and before lunch. Don't forget to bring your brother,' said Mrs Harris.

I thought, she can't harm us in hospital or pay us back for what we said, and we may learn what really happened at last. Suddenly I felt my spirits rising.

'Okay, we'll be there, I promise,' I said. 'Even if we have to walk.'

'Goodbye then,' said Mrs Harris, sounding even more disagreeable.

I put down the receiver. 'It's fantastic, absolutely fantastic,' I cried, going back to the kitchen. 'Mary wants me and Ben to visit her in hospital tomorrow.'

'They won't let you in. You're too young,' said Mummy.

'What for?' cried Ben.

'To make her peace. She's a good kid really,' said Dad, giving her the benefit of the doubt again.

I sat down.

Dad told Lisa, Georgie and Phillipa to go to bed. Paul was still reading *Horse and Hound*.

'We must go,' I said. 'She's got special permission.'

'I'll take you,' offered Dad, 'because I think she needs help.'

'Don't we all?' asked James.

'Exactly,' agreed Mummy.

'She probably wants to say she's sorry,' said Ben.

'Or tell her side of the story and it had better be good,' I answered. 'Because she's caused plenty of misery one way and another.'

'We all make mistakes,' replied Dad.

'I want to hear her story anyway, and I want to say I'm sorry, too,' I answered.

Outside it was dark. It had been a long day. The morning seemed already to belong to another life. I thought, soon we'll be back at school. And I don't remember anything from last term, not a word of French nor a line of English. It all seems so small compared to life. What does the French for chimney-stack matter compared with Apollo dead in a wood, or Mary with her leg broken? I thought, I shall never cope, never concentrate again and Miss Pitts will be furious and I shall be hauled before the headmaster.

I struggled to my feet. My legs felt heavy and suddenly I was tired beyond words. 'I'm going to bed,' I said.

Mummy was telling Ben to clean his nails and wash his hair. 'They don't like dirty people in hospital,' she said. 'Sister won't let you in.'

James was making himself yet another cup of coffee.

'I'm going to bed, too,' Paul said.

He had dark circles under his eyes, but he wasn't crying any more.

'Sleep well,' said Mrs Mills. 'I'm on my way as well. I'm just going to fill my hot water bottle first.'

Phillipa and Georgie had put themselves to bed leaving a note

82

on my pillow which read: 'We hate Mary and love you. P and G.' I thought that I didn't deserve it, that I didn't help anyone enough and had made a muddle of telling Paul about Apollo. In fact, one way and another, I was a bit of a failure. There was a moon outside now, looking wild and free in the sky, and the village looked shadowy and romantic like something in a film.

The hours in the wood and finding Apollo dead seemed impossible as I undressed and got into bed, and I thought, whatever happens tomorrow can't be worse than today or yesterday.

Nine
Mary tells her story

The next morning was wild and windy. I had slept badly, dreaming of Mary throwing bricks at Ben. There was a pile of letters on the hall mat when I wandered downstairs still half asleep. Mrs Mills appeared and held out a hand. She was always hoping for a letter from her daughter, which never came.

'Sorry. Nothing,' I said now, saddened by her disappointed face.

It was like any other morning except for our impending visit to the hospital hanging over everything. I dressed and ran round to the stables. It was still early and everything smelt lovely, full of hope and rising sap, new leaves, growing grass; there seemed no room for sorrow or regrets. I found Paul already there, leaning on the field gate.

'You're early,' I said. 'Couldn't you sleep?'

'No, not a wink,' he answered. 'Say, there's a sale of horses next week. How about going? It's in the same county as here.' He had *Horse and Hound* in his pocket and he unfolded it now and read: "300 horses and ponies; 150 lots of saddlery and harness, etc." There's sure to be something suitable and I don't want to wait,' he added.

I knew how he felt, how he hated waiting, how we seemed to be doing nothing, though Apollo had been dead for two days. I could understand his impatience, but buying a horse in a hurry is apt to lead to disaster, or so the experts say.

'It's in three days' time,' he continued, 'and some of them are warranted, so we needn't get another one like Apollo.'

'Buying a horse in a sale is always a risk,' I said, feeling mean.

'I know Lorraine came from one, but we knew her history.'

I ran my eye over our ponies without really seeing them, but I knew they were all right, without strains or sprains or colic or anything else.

'Can we look at some anyway?' insisted Paul.

'Okay, if there's any transport. But I want to improve your riding first; otherwise we'll have to get something solid and quiet because we don't want any more accidents,' I said.

We went back to the house together, and I set the table for breakfast and woke my parents with a cup of tea.

Dad didn't go to the factory any more. He had paid his workers large sums of money to compensate them for losing their jobs, but no one had paid him anything. Once he had risen before any of us, but this morning he wasn't up till nine and then he sat for ages simply sipping coffee.

Paul read *Horse and Hound* all through breakfast, marking advertisements with a pen.

'I want to call up Dad later to ask how much we can spend,' he said, looking round the breakfast table.

'I'm afraid we can't advance you a thousand pounds,' replied Dad quickly. 'But call up your dad by all means. James will put you through.'

'I'm just checking your clothes for school. You've only got five more days here,' Mummy said.

The holidays were almost over. I went away to get ready for hospital. I was longing to hear Mary's side of the story, to know what had really happened. But would she tell us the truth?

The hospital smelt of antiseptic. Ben had put on his new coat and brushed his hair until it lay like polished, flattened straw across his forehead. I had put on jodhpurs because my trousers were either dirty or frayed or far too short. I had put on jodhpur boots, too, and my best polo-necked jersey.

Mary lay in a long ward full of old ladies with broken limbs. She sat propped up with pillows, looking young and fragile.

A nurse said, 'Now don't stay long, and don't upset Mary, she's still suffering from exposure and shock.'

'Okay,' said Ben grinning.

The old ladies stared at us as though we were strangers from outer space. I felt hideously self-conscious in my riding clothes.

Mary waved a wan hand in our direction. 'Come and sit down', she called. We found two chairs and sat on them.

'Are you better?' asked Ben.

'How do you feel?' I inquired at the same moment.

'All right. But what about Apollo? Mummy didn't say a thing. Why did he die? What did the vet say? Was it my fault?'

Ben shook his head. 'He died of a tumour; that's why he was so sleepy when he came. We should have realized, but we didn't. He didn't look round or neigh or anything – remember? He was going to die anyway. Roy says he must have been seized by a frenzy, that's why he galloped and wouldn't stop,' continued Ben.

'Sssh, you're keeping the ward awake,' said a nurse. 'It's rest time, you know, talk softly.'

'Sorry. He must have gone on till he hit that tree and then had a fit. That what Roy says? Is that right?' continued Ben, lowering his voice.

Mary nodded. 'I thought it was my fault,' she whispered. 'I've done so many awful things. I thought that it was just one more. I've been so miserable. I just wanted to die.'

'What really happened?' I asked.

'Begin at the beginning,' suggested Ben. 'Why did you get up in the middle of the night?'

'I heard the horses neighing. I wasn't really asleep. I was dreaming about Trixie. She was lost and I was looking for her and for a time I thought it was Trixie and then suddenly I knew where I was.

'I leapt out of bed and pulled on some trousers and a pullover. There was a horsebox by the gate with its lights on, and men in the yard. I shouted, "Get out, clear off, I've called the police." All the gates were open. I was terribly scared really. My knees were knocking. I heard someone throw up a ramp, the roar of an engine, and then suddenly the box was gone.'

'And the ponies?' asked Ben, leaning forward in his chair. 'Where were they?'

'All the gates were open. The box must have been backed up to the yard entrance,' continued Mary. 'And by the time I got there the ponies were thundering away across the common. Of course I should have gone back to the house then and raised the alarm, but I didn't. I wanted to show you I was all right really, to make amends. So I tacked up Apollo and went in pursuit and that's when it happened – he went mad. I pulled and pulled, I even yelled. He went round and round in circles and then suddenly straight for the woods like something possessed. I tried to steer him into trees to stop him but he just went on until he fell . . . '

'And had a fit,' finished Ben. 'That's how Roy said it would have happened.'

'I wanted to make a good impression to save the ponies,' said Mary wearily, wiping a tear from her eye. 'You won't believe it, but I did. I know I'm objectionable. I don't like being the way I am, but I can't stop myself.'

'We are all like that sometimes,' Ben said in a voice I had never heard before.

'But what about Paul?' asked Mary. 'Is he very upset? Are his parents blaming you?'

'Roy, our vet, did a post-mortem. Everything is all right. Don't worry,' Ben replied, in a soothing voice which made me feel out on a limb suddenly.

'You don't understand, I love horses. I always have and I always will. It's mother who doesn't like them. She says they give her hay fever. I think it's just an excuse to keep away. She doesn't like me either,' continued Mary.

'She must,' I said, 'she's your mother.'

'It doesn't follow. Don't be a fool, Harriet. All mothers don't love their children,' replied Ben.

'Most do,' I said, 'it's natural.'

'It was all right until Trixie went,' continued Mary. 'I was quite a nice person until that happened. Nothing has been the same since then. When she went I wanted to die.'

'What happened?' I asked.

Mary looked away. Ben frowned at me and I knew he was thinking that I was tactless, but I wanted to know, now before Mary was gone for ever.

'It's a long story,' she began. 'Dad bought her for me on my ninth birthday. I remember when she came. It was so lovely. He brought her right into the kitchen and she ate oats off the kitchen table. She was grey like Lorraine, but smaller, and she was the first pony I had ever had.'

The bossy nurse came back. 'Only five more minutes,' she hissed.

Ben made a face at her back. 'Go on,' he said.

'Then a year later Mummy and Daddy broke up. They had been quarrelling for years. Daddy simply got fed up and went off with someone else, right away to South Africa.'

'How awful,' I said.

'It was such a long way, I knew it was final. I blamed Mummy. I couldn't forgive her. She sent me away to a boarding school. I remember it so well. I was all dressed up in some ghastly uniform' – Mary was crying openly now – 'and the last thing I said was, "Look after Trix, won't you? Two full haynets a day and two feeds, don't forget." I wanted to say goodbye to Trixie once more, but Mummy wouldn't wait, she said we were late already. She said, "Don't worry, I'll look after her, I promise." Then when I came back she was gone. Mummy had sent her to the market, she said she couldn't afford the food for her now that Daddy had deserted us and I should blame him, but the cocktail cupboard was full of drink and the deep freeze was full of steak and you know what that costs,' finished Mary.

I tried to think of something to say.

Ben said, 'Why didn't she find her a nice home or lend her to someone?'

'She couldn't be bothered, that's why,' replied Mary bitterly. 'It would have meant seeing people, explaining, and she doesn't know the first thing about ponies. So you see I hate both my parents. Daddy for going away and leaving me and Mummy for selling Trix. And I hated you too,' she continued, 'because you had all the things I had lost – two parents, ponies, the lot.'

'Perhaps we could find Trixie,' I replied, feeling hopelessly inadequate to the situation.

'She went for meat. They all did that month, there was a hay shortage and a meat shortage and it was half-way through the winter, the worst time to sell a pony. And Trixie was only entered as "Grey pony" in the catalogue, nothing about being good or kind or a lovely ride. Mummy was too lazy or too ignorant to put anything else. That's my mother for you,' finished Mary.

Most of the old ladies in the ward were asleep by this time.

I imagined Mary coming home from boarding school, finding the paddock empty, running to the house shouting, 'Where's Trixie?' I wondered how I would have felt.

'Then I met Ted. Here, I've got a photograph of him,' said Mary, putting a hand under her pillow. 'His parents are separated too. We discuss our situations. He's the only person I can really talk to – you see he knows what it feels like to be me. I didn't really run away, Mummy invented that. She knows I talk about her to Ted, that's why.'

I looked at the photograph. Ted was dark-haired with a kind, square-shaped face. He looked like a person you could trust.

'He looks nice,' I said. 'And good-tempered too,' I added, passing the photograph to Ben.

But now two or three nurses rushed into the ward and started straightening bedclothes. The old ladies sat up dazed and one asked, 'What is it, nurse? What's happening?'

'It's the consultant, he's come,' replied a nurse.

And we knew we would have to go in a minute. And we hadn't said half the things we wanted to say. A nurse started straightening Mary's bed. 'How do you feel, dear?' she asked.

'Better, much better.'

'You two must go now,' the nurse said. 'The doctors are on their way. And it's the consultant's morning.'

'Just one more minute,' pleaded Mary.

'Just one then, but keep your voices down,' replied the nurse.

'I don't want to go home,' announced Mary, looking straight at Ben. 'Will you have me back? I will help, I promise. I will be like Mrs Mills. I'll make the beds and wash up, and groom the ponies and muck out. Mummy's going to marry someone I hate and they won't want me around – please.'

I couldn't imagine Mary making beds or washing up or being like Mrs Mills.

I looked at Ben. We could see a sister coming into the ward now. Ben looked as though he wanted to say yes, but he didn't dare speak for our parents, he had to ask first. Mary grabbed his hand. 'Please . . .' she said, as though that one word could melt a heart of stone.

'Can't you wait a few hours?' asked Ben.

Mary shook her head. 'Mummy's bringing my clothes this afternoon. They want the bed. I've told everyone I'm going to you. I was sure you would say yes, when you knew the truth.'

I thought of her lying upstairs, being waited on, getting better. She might change and become nasty again. How could we tell? But Ben was on his feet now. 'I'll go and ask Dad, he's outside waiting for us,' he said. 'I can't say yes on my own.'

And I knew what Dad's answer would be for he couldn't turn a wounded fly away, much less Mary. He simply wasn't tough enough.

'You don't mind, do you? I don't mind where I sleep. And Mummy will keep on paying, she gets loads of alimony,' Mary continued as though it was settled already.

'I'm sorry about Trixie. It must have been awful,' I said. 'And I'm sorry we called you such awful names.'

'It doesn't matter. I can go to the local school, can't I?' I nodded. I wondered what Mummy would say when we told her. The doctors were coming nearer every moment. I stood up. Ben came back smiling, followed by three nurses buzzing round him like angry bees.

'It's all fixed up,' he said.

'Out,' said one of the nurses. 'Out at once.'

Mary smiled at us.

'See you later,' Ben said.

'Mummy's going to un-stop the cheque. I made her,' Mary said.

'Out,' hissed the nurse. 'You shouldn't be in here, the consultant's here.'

Outside the air was fresh and free and sunlit. Dad was smiling in the car. 'I knew she was a good kid,' he said. 'Just a bit mixed up.'

'We don't seem to have lost a single guest after all,' I said. 'I just hope she doesn't change back to how she was before.'

'Change back?'

'To how she was three days ago,' I answered.

We told Dad what Mary had said on the way home.

The house looked peaceful when we reached it. Mrs Mills was weeding a border and Mummy's new help had come and was shaking mats. James was practising driving the Land Rover and Lisa was jumping Jigsaw, watched by Paul, Phillipa and Georgie.

'She meant well,' said Ben, getting out of the car. 'And she was jolly brave going out alone to face the horse thieves.' And I thought that he was like Dad, always willing to give anyone the benefit of a doubt. 'She probably saved them too,' he added.

'I'll break it to your mother. I'm sure she'll be pleased,' Dad said.

We had been through a kind of hell and yet nothing was really changed. The house looked the same, and the stables; only Apollo was missing and Mary's leg would have to mend, otherwise all was the same – the flowers were still growing, the trees still stood where they had always stood.

I could hear Mummy laughing as I went inside.

'So she's coming back after all,' she said. 'And we have all these other people who want to come. Let's go through the letters together. We can pick and choose our guests now. Isn't it fantastic?'

'No more neurotic girls, please,' said James, coming in with the sun behind him.

'No more sick horses,' I added. 'I can't bear another death.'

'There's a colonel,' began Mummy, 'who wants to look after the garden for a small reduction. He's ninety-two. And there's a strange man who calls himself Commander Cooley; and a family of five with Mum expecting another who want a rest. They want reductions because all the children are under ten and Dad knows about horses and can drive.'

'They all sound strange,' I said. 'And we've had enough of strangers already. No one could have been stranger than Mary was.'

'Or poor sick Apollo,' added Ben.

'Or the Armstrongs paying all that money for a dying horse,' said Dad.

'And then there's one from a social worker who wants us to take on a delinquent boy who loves horses; and there're three children who need a foster mother. And five horses who need a home for six months,' answered Mummy.

'We'll take the horses,' cried Ben.

Mummy put down the letters. 'I have been writing up a guests' charter,' she said. 'Two in fact – one to hang in the hall, the other to be signed by adults when they leave their charges here. We should have thought of it before. Listen.'

She started to read and it took me back to my infancy when she used to read aloud to us before we lived in our present house.

ALL GUESTS TO HAVE BREAKFAST BY 9.30 AM
ALL CHILDREN UNDER FOURTEEN TO BE IN BED BY 9.30 PM

'That's too early,' yelled Ben.

ALL CHILDREN TO WEAR SUITABLE HARD HATS WHEN RIDING
ALL RIDERS TO LEAVE WRITTEN NOTICE OF WHERE THEY ARE GOING WHEN HACKING
ALL PONIES TO BE BROUGHT HOME COOL
ALL DIRTY SHOES TO BE LEFT IN LOBBY OR SCULLERY
ALL NIGHT CLOTHES TO BE LEFT ON CHAIR OR BED
NO CLOTHES TO BE LEFT ON FLOORS
ALL BATHROOMS TO BE LEFT AS FOUND

She stopped for breath. 'Anything else?'

'I'll think,' said Dad.

'The other one is more legal. It must be signed, it's all about not holding us responsible for death, illness, theft, injury etc, etc. And about children coming here at their own risk. I'll get it copied if you are all agreeable.'

'Let's get a solicitor to look at it first,' suggested Dad.

'Someone telephoned this morning about your having two ponies to get fit before camp,' continued Mummy, looking at Ben and me. 'They want you to name a price,' she said.

'In or out?'

'I didn't ask. Here's the number.'

'Everything is going to be all right, isn't it?' I said, taking the number which was on a scrap of paper. 'We can go on being a guest house?'

Mummy nodded. 'And we can choose our guests now,' she said.

Lisa, Phillipa, Georgie and Paul were coming towards the house, pushing each other and laughing. Mrs Mills waved her trowel at them and called, 'Keep off the flower beds.'

There was sunlight everywhere. I watched them coming without really seeing them, seeing instead new guests, strange ponies coming, strange riders. I hoped we would choose well.

'Isn't it lovely to sit and know everything's all right after all,' said Ben. 'That Mary's coming back and that Paul's staying, that we've succeeded in spite of everything.'

'It's a miracle,' James said. 'And I vote we have the old Colonel, because I'm sick of mowing the lawn.'

'No. I want Commander Cooley. He sounds like MI5,' said Ben.

'There isn't any hurry to decide,' Mummy said. 'Tomorrow will do.'

'There goes the telephone again,' James cried. 'And that will be another one.'

'Perhaps we should take the delinquent boy,' said Mummy. 'It might make all the difference to him.'

'It's people wanting to come for the weekend,' said James, coming back. 'Two children who are mad about riding and two parents who are mad about walking, three dogs and a tortoise.'

But whom we took next and how Mary behaved, and what pony we bought for Paul belong to another book.

Also by Christine Pullein-Thompson

Christine Pullein-Thompson's **Book of Pony Stories** 40p

An anthology of pony stories from many well-known writers. You will find all sorts of pony stories – sad, exciting, funny, even ghostly. You meet a cart horse, a farm horse, horses from Australia, ponies from the pony club and many others.

If you love ponies and horses you will be thrilled by this new collection from Christine Pullein-Thompson.

A Pony to Love 35p

Do you want a pony of your own?
Or do you already have one?

Whichever it is, this book is a basic and detailed guide to everything you need to know about buying, owning, feeding and keeping a pony. It is invaluable and fascinating for all pony lovers, and is enlivened by cartoons throughout.